THE FIRST TIME . . .

I met Steve at the beach on a hot June Saturday at the end of my junior year in high school. Only a year older than me, he seemed much more sure of himself. He was tall and slender, fair skinned—reddening when I met him—with blond hair even lighter than mine.

He was at the beach with a couple of friends. I was there with a girl I knew from school, but his friends didn't come over to our blanket. Only Steve sat with me, smoking seriously and regarding me with an obvious sexual interest that hit me below my stomach.

Suddenly, he asked, "Anyone home in your house now?"

"No. My mother works. She comes home about six."

"Come on. Let's go, I'll take you home."

While he went to get his things, I put on my clothes. My girlfriend told me I was crazy to go with him. "He's only interested in what he can get out of you," she told me.

"Don't say that," I protested. "He's nice."

"Then why did he ask you if anyone's home?"

She was right, of course. It was better to be stupid than fast, so I pretended to be stupid.

We necked on the subway going home. He tasted of salt and sand. When we got to my house it was only four. We had plenty of time. He stepped out of his pants gingerly and asked me where my bed was. I led him to my room.

"I—I'm a virgin," I told him, sitting on the bed. I don't know if he believed me. He slipped down his bathing suit and I removed mine—then I closed my eyes and waited . . .

All The Way

By
Felice Buckvar

ZEBRA BOOKS

KENSINGTON PUBLISHING CORP.

ZEBRA BOOKS

are published by

KENSINGTON PUBLISHING CORP.
21 East 40th Street
New York, N.Y. 10016

TO MY MOTHER

Friday Night

Opening the car door, I counted to myself for what must have been the fiftieth time that day. I was six days overdue. My period was six days late.

The heat inside the auto was stifling. The seat had been in the sun and it was burning hot. I raised myself, but then lowered my butt again. I'd have to get used to it. It was time to go home.

I flicked on the air conditioner and opened the window. I wasn't nauseous, not yet, but I did feel uncomfortable. It felt as though my period were about to come on. That was the way I felt in the early months with Barry some eighteen years ago.

Eighteen years ago! Maybe I was due to give birth every eighteen years. The next time around I would be how old? Eighteen and thirty-six. Fifty-four.

Just leave it to me, I thought. If I could get pregnant at thirty-six, unmarried, I guess I'd be able to manage it at fifty-four.

I pulled away from the curb. Thirty-six seemed closer to fifty-four than eighteen. Now why was that? I wondered.

I was driving out of the business district into the section of highway devoted to cars. Countless numbers stood in open lots, row upon row of gleaming metal. And when they were bought, any part of them could be replaced from this very same stretch. There were stores for mufflers, motors, transmissions, slipcovers, brakes, radios, tires; places to have the car painted, washed, simonized, repaired in any way imaginable. In towns for commuters, the cars were as important as homes.

Home. The thought of mine was a relief. It would be good to get home. I had spent the better part of an hour unsuccessfully trying to straighten out an order of lamps for a customer. I was tired and hungry and upset.

I'll go home and make supper for Barry and me. Another thought occurred to me: I hope Suzanne isn't there.

I tried to remember what Barry had told me in the morning. He did say something about going out with Suzanne and some other kids. Damn it.

And the fluttering feeling, the worry, returned. It was worse than the heat. Worse than being pregnant at thirty-six years of age. It was a feeling of helplessness. Suzanne brought it on as she always did. Always.

She was only three when I first saw her. Nat brought her to the office with him one day. Suzanne, the boss's daughter. She was thin and dark, mousy, and, being shy, she was awkward. But I knew enough to fuss over her.

I didn't see her again for months until one warm spring Sunday. Nat's divorce was almost final and he had Suzanne for the day. We all went to the zoo.

I must have seemed old to her although I was only about eighteen myself. An only child, I didn't know what to say to that little mole of a girl. It hardly mattered. Nat was too excited to notice anything.

"Look at her. Look at her. Isn't she a doll?"

He had used those words to describe me as well as his daughter. She didn't know if he meant her. I didn't know if he meant me.

We walked, the three of us. The air was heavy with the smells of the zoo. Cotton candy, hay, animals, and new grass mingled and blended. Of the three of us, Nat seemed most excited. Suzanne appeared uninterested and my high heels were killing me. Who wanted to go to a lousy zoo anyway?

"Are you hungry? Want a frank? A soda?"

Before I could answer, Nat was looking around for the next thing to do.

We came to the merry-go-round. Suzanne was going to go on.

"You want to go on, too?" he asked me.

I would have if his daughter weren't with us, but now it seemed silly. I shook my head. "I'll wait," I said.

Nat went on to hold her. The lights flashed, the music tinkled, and Nat waved every time he passed me, but the little girl on the horse never waved or laughed or even smiled.

Later when Nat went to the men's room, I was left alone with her. It was an awkward few minutes for me. I knew that at home she was probably being taught to hate me. Her mother was a first-class bitch, Nat told me, and a liar. Anyway, I had a ring on my finger, a diamond solitaire, and I didn't have to worry about pleasing Suzanne, not anymore. Someday maybe I wouldn't have to see her at all, but till then I'd smile and try to be pleasant, and that should be enough. After all, the only thing we had in common was that we both wanted Nat for our very own.

And now Barry, I realized, for it hadn't worked out as I had planned. For years at a time, Suzanne was out of my life, but she came back like a chronic infection.

She was a woman of twenty-two now, all

nervous movements and jerks, cigarette smoke and long tangled hair. She was bright and bitchy with the brutal honesty of someone who doesn't have to work for a living or even show up at a school. Luckily for her, she had a rich stepfather. She could do what she was best at—bumming around.

Unfortunately, my son was one of the kids she bummed around with. The last time I begged Barry to stop seeing so much of her, he had answered me angrily.

"She's my sister. You'll never separate us."

I could hear Suzanne's voice in those words. For his sake, I put up with all her crises big and small, and there were some whoppers. He felt responsible for her. Since he was twelve, he had tried to take care of his older half sister. Who else but Suzanne could even use a twelve-year-old protector?

I turned into my block. Sure enough, there was Suzanne's car in front of my house. It stood a good eighteen inches from the curb, its front pointed to the lawn, its back in the path of traffic.

It had been parked there yesterday, too, when I got home. Barry had been in the

14

kitchen doing some homework.

"Where is she?" I had asked him.

"She's sleeping."

My expression must have changed.

"She's tired," he explained.

Later when I went into his room, she was sleeping in his bed in her bra and panties. My heart sank.

I tried watching Barry to see if he were acting any differently. I couldn't tell.

In a way, he reminded me of my father. My father died when I was a kid and although I knew the way he read the paper—neatly, from the first page to the last—and the way he cut up his food—he cut it all up into tiny pieces before he started eating—there were vast deserts and oases in his life I knew nothing about until years later. I couldn't even guess at them. And now I didn't know the most important things about my son, either.

As I pulled my car into the driveway past Suzanne's for the second day in a row, I tried to steel myself for my stepdaughter. Oh, but she got under my skin. How hard was it to park the car the right way? Why did she have to be such a jerk in everything she did?

"Hello?" I called out, warning them that I was in the house. But when I looked upstairs from the center hall, they were both on the living-room couch, Barry sitting further away from the door, Suzanne lying on her back, her head in Barry's lap.

"Hi, Ma."

"Hello, Barry, Suzanne."

She glanced at me, but she didn't answer.

I went up the steps into the living room. At least her shoes were off. Her feet had a border of black around them.

She was wearing a halter and a pair of jeans. Barry was in dungarees and a T-shirt.

"Is she all right?" Or is she drunk, stoned, strung out, or whatever else they call it?

"She's all right, Ma." Barry spoke of her gently, with love in his voice. His hand lay softly on her hair.

What was he doing—a seventeen-year-old—on a summer's day with his half-sister's head in his lap. Other boys his age were playing basketball. They were at the beach. . . .

"Suzanne. Will you please get up! I want to speak to you."

I hadn't planned on getting angry. It was

just that everything she did irked me. Like now. The way she closed her eyes and turned her head away from me, deeper into Barry's lap.

"Suzanne. Will you sit up?"

I couldn't help the way I sounded. Better to express anger anyway. If I held it in, it would only churn and burn in my stomach.

Suzanne opened her eyes and turned her head to look at me. She didn't move to get up. Barry shook the shock of black hair out of his eyes.

"I can't talk to her when she's lying like that," I told him.

"Why are you angry, Ma?" he asked me in his sad, complaining voice. Just like Nat, I thought.

His deep-blue eyes looked troubled. They were such beautiful eyes, framed with long black lashes. They were from my side. My Aunt Shirley had eyes like that.

He was waiting for my answer.

"Don't you know?" I replied.

He didn't.

"You better get up," he said to Suzanne, moving his leg, and Suzanne, disturbed, sat up slowly, yawning. She was still leaning against him, but, finally, her feet were on the rug.

I had to say what was on my mind. Perhaps if I could sound friendly . . . .

"Listen, kids, I'll tell you why I'm so uptight with you."

Stretching for her cigarettes on the table, Suzanne glanced at me with an amused pout on her lips. I could read her thoughts. She always unnerved me, and she knew it.

"All right," I conceded. "Why *now* more than ever."

"What are you trying to tell us, Phyllis?" she asked.

"I . . ." No. That wasn't the way to start. I focused on Barry. It was easier to speak to him. "Barry, Suzanne is a half-sister. That's still a sister. Don't do anything wrong with her."

I could see he didn't understand what I was trying to say.

"I mean—sexually."

Suzanne giggled. She stood shaking her head.

"You know what she means. She means I-N-C-E-S-T. Incest. Get it?"

Again she giggled, and Barry, watching her, reddened. His cheeks puffed out as though he were trying not to laugh, and then the laugh burst out. Suzanne was laughing hysterically, choking on her smoke, coughing and laughing.

"What's so hilarious?" Was it too late? Was that the joke? God forbid.

"What the hell are you two laughing about?"

Suzanne stopped first. She turned to Barry, wiping the tears from her face and sniffling.

"Why don't you tell her?" she asked him. "Go on. Tell her." She waved her cigarette at him as if she were leading him with it. "She's got to know sometime."

He stopped laughing, holding his bottom lip with his teeth.

"You want me to tell her?" Suzanne asked him.

He nodded.

"Phyllis," Suzanne began, her voice higher, excited. "Barry would never go for a sister. Maybe a *brother* . . ."

She was talking and glancing from Barry to me. Barry looked pained. I didn't know what the hell she was trying to get at.

"Phyllis, I'm trying to tell you that Barry and I are safe with one another. He likes boys."

Likes boys? He was shy with girls, that's true. He liked Suzanne. What the hell did she mean?

Barry stood. I still wasn't used to his height. He towered over me, my father's height.

"Ma," he began, his voice a husky croak. "I'm a homosexual."

Homosexual . . . I put a hand on my stomach. I was feeling sick, after all.

Suzanne stepped near him, leaning forward with him, smoking and coughing. Again, she brought trouble. Again.

"Suzanne. See your baby brother? Isn't he cute? You love him. Go. Kiss his little hand."

Nat brought her to the house every Sunday. Every Sunday I had to put up with her dark looks, her silent reproaches.

Yet Nat brought her and pushed the baby on her as though he had never heard of sibling rivalry. As though he couldn't read the hate on her face.

He took care of her as I busied myself with Barry. Cutting up her food he would coo, "Come on, little buttercup. Eat your yummy green peas."

It was enough to make me puke.

Hints didn't work with him. He loved to boast how wonderfully Suzanne and I got along and how she adored her baby half-brother, and I was in no position to tell him differently.

Suddenly, I was wealthy. I was important as Mrs. Albert. I could do anything I wanted, but certain things were expected of me. I had to put up with Suzanne. But there were ways.

How much did I love that perfect little baby of mine? He was beautiful, with a round face and bright blue eyes, shining brown hair. I could sit and watch him for hours. But did I love him as much as I disliked Suzanne?

I knew what would happen if I left her alone with him. Barry was my wedge against her.

The telephone rang one Sunday after lunch. Nat picked it up in our bedroom. I didn't have to follow him, but I put Barry in his crib and left Suzanne with him.

It was only one of Nat's salesmen calling. I waited, listening. Just as Nat put down the receiver, the baby let out a scream. We ran to his room. Suzanne was standing near the crib. In her hand was Barry's silver brush.

The baby was tensed up and red with screaming. Across the fingers of his right hand was a line, the mark of a blow.

"What happened?" Nat demanded of her. "Did you hit him?"

"His fingers," I cried.

Nat touched the fingers that the baby held out flat. Barry's scream intensified.

"We'll take him to the emergency room. You get him dressed. I'll get the car." He turned to Suzanne. "You come with me."

In the car, he questioned his daughter. Whimpering, she nodded her confession.

"You hit him? Your own brother?" Nat seemed amazed.

"Just drive," I told him. "Pay attention to the road."

One finger was broken. (It would never heal properly. Somehow Barry always managed to hurt that finger when he played ball; and when he tried to build something or tie a knot, that bent finger always got in his way.)

The finger was taped with shining white tape making it look like a giant's finger next to that little doll-like body. I put a sleeping Barry back in his crib. When I came into the kitchen, Nat was shouting at Suzanne.

"How could you do it? How could you do it?"

He had her by the shoulders and he shook her, her head bobbing loosely, the fear in her dark eyes.

"No!" I came between them. "Don't hurt her. She's only a child. But, Nat, for Barry's sake, don't bring her here anymore."

"Of course not." He pulled Suzanne out of the room. "Come. Get your jacket."

I had won. For weeks the bandaged finger reminded me of my victory. It would always be misshapen, but I had gotten rid of Nat's daughter.

One night I lay awake in bed, Nat snoring beside me no matter how many times I elbowed and shook him, and I thought of Suzanne. Suddenly I realized that it could have been Barry's head as well as his finger. I jumped out of bed and went to Barry's room to kiss him. I sat in the rocking chair next to his crib for hours watching him sleep and weeping with love and with guilt.

*   *   *

Now Suzanne was here again, upsetting my life, making trouble.

"She's always been trouble for you," I said to Barry. "Right, Suzanne?" I was stepping toward her. My words made no logical sense, I knew, and yet I felt that they were right.

She snickered at me, snorting through her nose. "Really, Phyllis."

Barry stepped between us. Why did he look as though he were on the verge of tears?

I stopped and stared at him.

"Ma," he said.

What did he tell me before? A homosexual. At seventeen? Wasn't it too young to know? Maybe he was just late in developing.

"Did you ever . . . I mean, are you a virgin, Barry?"

His lips tightened and he shook his head. "No."

"You're not a virgin?" I could see myself as though from afar. I knew I wasn't making complete sense yet the words spewed uncontrollably. "When did all this happen, Barry? I mean, you never even started going out with girls, and now you say you had sex with a boy and you're queer!"

He hung his head like a little child hurt. Well, how else should I say it?

I couldn't stop. "Answer me! How did you become queer? That's all I want to know."

Everything sensible in me said *no*, but my blood was pulsing hot and fast through my head. I had to do something or burst. I lifted my hand. I slapped him once, hard. My palm stung.

The last time I had hit him like that was when he was a child of nine. He was obedient and helpful, but he couldn't take punishment. His slightest misdeed would mushroom as I tried to punish him and he rebelled against the punishment.

I hit him that time and he pushed me back, almost instinctively, bowling me over. In terror, he ran away. He was gone for hours. I didn't say anything to him when he returned. The whole incident was over nothing and I vowed never to hit him again. I hadn't—till now.

He turned to Suzanne, the mark from my fingers imprinted on his cheek, his eyes shining.

"Come on," he said to her. "Let's get out

of here."

He ran out of the house without looking back while she put on her sandals and tucked her cigarettes into her waistband. At the door, she stopped and turned to me as if to say, You fucked this one up, Phyllis. And then she was gone.

I could hear the car pull away outside. When I went to the window to look, they had already turned the corner. Only the stale smell of cigarette smoke and an open book of matches on the table advertising "Be a Computer Programmer" remained of their presence.

"Damn him," I said out loud. "And damn her. The freaks!"

I glanced at the clock on the wall, a handsome grandmother clock rimmed with the blue of the Oriental rug on the floor. It was seven o'clock. And it was almost the seventh day my period was overdue.

The house was empty without them. I cleaned out the ashtray Suzanne had left full of butts and straightened the throw pillows they had tossed on the floor. When the living room was back to its usual perfect state—after all, I was a decorator and took pride in my home—I went into the kitchen to mix a drink.

Homosexual. I couldn't get the word out of my mind.

The phone rang. Who could it be? I pictured Steve as I went to get it and hoped it was him. It was my mother.

She asked about Barry and I told her he was fine. She started talking about her latest ache. I held the phone away from my ear. When I listened in again, she was speaking about her sister.

"She's back in the hospital. Her circulation is bad."

"Aunt Shirley?"

"Yes. For a woman just past sixty, her arteries are very bad, I understand. Well, maybe it's God's way of punishing her for all her whoring around."

I made a face at my drink. When my mother started cursing her sister, it was time to hang up.

"I'll call you on Sunday, Ma."

"All right. And kiss Barry for me."

"Sure."

Barry. I hung up the phone. Why did she have to remind me? I usually spoke to her about his good qualities, how mature he was and handsome and sweet. Maybe they were faults.

I took a frozen turkey pie out of the freezer. Glue and spice, that's what it tasted like. I would have cooked if Barry were home. I put the pie in the oven and sat waiting for it to brown.

Seventeen years. He was queer at seventeen. Experienced, yet. I sat back and tried to remember what I was like at that age. I remembered. By the time I was seventeen, I wasn't a virgin either.

I wasn't exactly fast for the times, and I wasn't a shy wallflower. From about thirteen when I started going out with boys until I met Steve, I had a nice routine, safe and satisfying.

Feel me up for your pleasure. I just didn't get any thrill when you touched my breasts. Feel me down for mine. Rub gently, please, at first, and then as I became moister, harder for a second, and ah, that was good.

For a reward, you could press against me. Yes, lie on top of me with your clothes on and with mine. Pump. It wasn't the most comfortable position, but when you came to a climax all I would feel was your forward thrust. No mess, no bother. You had to wash first, that's all. Both of us were satisfied and my hymen was still intact, I think.

Recently, I read an article by a youngster who made fun of finger fucking. So it had a name. Finger fucking. Dry humping. Ugly names.

There were many boys, nice boys from school or from the neighborhood. They didn't lose respect for me, and at that time respect was as important as any thrill. I could still go up to them in the cafeteria at school and exchange desserts with them or work on a project with them for English without any embarrassment. They never joked about our dates or acted forward at the wrong times. They were my friends. And then I met Steve.

I met him at the beach on a hot June Saturday at the end of my junior year in high school. Only a year older than me, he seemed much more sure of himself. (Later I decided he just didn't give a damn.) He was tall and slender, fair skinned—reddening when I met him—with blond hair even lighter than mine.

He was at the beach with a couple of friends. I was there with a girl I knew from school, but his friends didn't come over to our blanket. Only Steve sat with me while my girl friend lay on the other edge of the blanket, annoyed. He smoked seriously and regarded me with an obvious sexual interest that hit me below my stomach.

I kept up a half-hearted conversation with him about where we lived and went to school.

Suddenly, he asked, "Anyone home in your house now?"

"No. My mother works. She comes home around six."

"Come on. Let's go. I'll take you home."

While he went to his blanket to get his things, I put on my shirt and dungarees. My girl friend told me I was crazy to go with him. We had seen some other girls from our school. I told her to sit with them. I knew this was the end of our friendship, but we were hardly friends anyway. She probably would have left me if anyone as attractive as Steve had asked her.

He was at his blanket wiping the sand off his body, shaking off his pants, and putting them on.

"He's only interested in what he can get out of you," she told me as she gathered her towels and lotion.

"Don't say that," I protested. "He's nice."

"Then why did he ask you if anyone's home?"

She was right, of course. It was better to be stupid than fast, so I pretended to be stupid. Anyway, she'd be gossiping with the girls from our school in minutes.

"He asked me to go out with him," I lied.

"Oh, yeah?"

"Yeah. When you went for the soda. I told him I'd have to check with my mother when she comes home."

He was at our blanket waiting for me.

Oh, hell, he was so good-looking and he had that forceful way about him. I don't think I'd have gone with him if he weren't Jewish. I'd be scared to, but he wore a Star of David around his neck. To hell with my girl friend!

We necked on the subway going home. He tasted of salt and sand. Once he put his arm around me. "Ouch!"

Once I moved closer to him. He moved his thigh. "Don't."

Under the subway lights, he was red. I was pink.

When we got to my house, it was only

four. We had plenty of time. I took off my outer things and stayed in my bathing suit even though it was moist and sandy. I asked him if he wanted talcum powder for his sunburn. He did, and I dusted my shoulders and my legs with it, too.

He stepped out of his pants gingerly. Standing in his bathing suit, his hard-on obvious beneath the stringy fibers, he asked me where my bed was. I led him into my bedroom.

"I—I'm a virgin," I told him, sitting on the bed. I don't know if he believed me.

"Doesn't your bathing suit hurt?" he asked me. "Come on. Take it off." He sounded annoyed at my slowness.

Obediently, I stripped.

He shook his head. "You're red. I don't want to hurt you. I'll put on a rubber." He smiled for the first time since we left the beach. "It's the only place we're not sunburned."

A rubber? That meant . . . All my care protecting it, only fingers before or through layers of clothing. He was getting the condom from his wallet. He came back to the room and slipped down his bathing suit grimacing. I closed my eyes and waited.

I felt a hand on my shoulder. "Ah-h-h!" I screamed.

"I'm sorry. On your side. It's the only way."

I turned on my side, facing him. He thrust it hot and thick into my pubic hair.

I moaned from the pain of his thighs against mine.

"Shut up. It hurts me, too." He put a hand on my backside. "Is that all right?" He stroked me from the back and thrust at me from the front.

The sunburn smarted. The penetration hurt. "Wait." I moved away.

"Come back," he said.

I came back. He put his fingers right above his penis and stroked me while he was in. Within seconds, he whispered, "Are you coming?"

"Uh-huh," I answered.

He flung himself against me.

Pain, smarting, orgasm, smell of ocean and sand and clean sheet.

He withdrew. I looked down. There was no bleeding. I touched myself there to be sure.

He patted the hair around my ear affectionately, careful not to let our bodies touch again. His first words were in a whisper. "Do you have any Noxzema in the house?"

Considering the fact that I was more than twice that age now and Steve was still my lover, it was an inauspicious beginning, I thought. I shook the cubes in my drink. But that was how it was for me when I was almost seventeen.

But of course I was no homo. What *did* he do? A picture of Barry naked in bed with my neighbor's son, a boy he played basketball with, came to mind. Did the other kid know? I wondered. They used to sit together for hours listening to tapes and records—with the door closed. Maybe the other kid was one, too. How could you tell?

There was a fairy in my high-school class. He minced and spoke effeminately, and he was beaten up regularly.

I remembered how one of the boys I dated would punch him every time he passed him. I objected once.

"Why don't you leave him alone?" I demanded.

"Him?" the boy had answered scornfully. "Don't stick up for him. You don't understand about fags. You can't understand."

And I wondered what horrible things the fairy wanted to do to straight boys to make them hate him so, things so horrible I as a girl couldn't conceive of them.

Barry, I thought, you could understand that fairy. Perhaps you could even love him.

Saturday

I was awakened by the telephone's ring on Saturday morning.

"Did I wake you?"

It was my mother, her voice husky. The clock read 8:05.

"Yes," I answered. "Is anything the

matter?"

"It's Aunt Shirley." She stopped speaking and cried into the phone. I knew what was coming. "She—she belongs to the ages."

Leave it to my mother to use an expression like that. "She's dead?"

"She passed away in the night."

Tears welled up filling my chest first and then my eyes. My mother was crying harder now.

"I can't believe it. My only sister. She was only sixty."

"Where's the funeral going to be?"

"Brooklyn. Tomorrow at eleven in the morning. Moe called. He's flying in with the body this morning. He'll be at the funeral home tonight. Will you come?"

I thought of Aunt Shirley. There was a time I felt closer to her than to my own mother.

"Of course," I answered. "Listen, Ma. Let me know when you're going to be there, and I'll meet you."

"All right." She sighed. "My sister. I hardly saw her since she moved to Florida. We didn't get along these last few years."

"I know, Ma. Don't let it worry you. She

had a good life."

"Yes."

I knew what she was thinking. She had said it often enough. *Too good for that whore.*

"I'll call you later." I hung up the phone and sobbed while I walked to the bathroom.

I went to check. Let me have my period, I thought. Nothing. The seventh day.

I washed, picturing the funeral ahead of me. I'd have to tell Barry about Aunt Shirley. Barry! How could I forget? Was he home?

I hit him. He was mad at me. There were tears in my eyes as I went to his room. I knew that if I were crying, it would be easier for me to handle him. Get his sympathy. Homo or not, we still had to put on an appearance for the rest of the world. But his room was empty.

There was a full ashtray, from Suzanne, no doubt, and the bedspread was creased as though someone had sat on it. I straightened it. The room was green, red, and brown with heavy, dark furniture. I had done the same room for several of my customers. It was so perfect for a boy, we all agreed.

Oh, damn it. Damn it. Damn it.

What did I say to him last night? Why did I have to hit him? These kids, I thought. They don't have to take what we took from our parents. They have choices we never dreamed of. Oh, where the hell is he?

I'd have to call Suzanne. There was nothing else I could do. I knew she had an apartment, but I didn't know where it was. I dialed Information.

There was no listing under Suzanne's name. I'd have to call Ruth to get the number. What a way to start the weekend.

Ruth thought of me as the man stealer who took Nat from her and her darling daughter. Man stealer. At eighteen. They could believe what they wanted, but the truth was that Ruth was better off without Nat than I was with him. And not only when she remarried a wealthier man, but from the beginning. She got a hundred and eighty dollars a week for nothing when Nat was alive. At the end, when Nat was running around trying to save his business, alternately hysterical and depressed, *I* envied *her*.

I dialed. Sure enough, Ruth answered.

I modulated my voice. "Hello. This is

Phyllis Albert. I'm sorry to be calling so early, but I've got to get in touch with my son. I think he's with Suzanne."

"They're not here." She sounded defensive.

Of course, they wouldn't be there. What was wrong with her? I used to think that Nat ran after me because I was irresistible. Anyone would seem good after her.

"I'm calling for Suzanne's telephone number at her apartment. They may be there." I could hardly recognize my own voice. It was so smooth, unctuous.

"Oh. Suzanne doesn't have a phone."

Of course not. Why should she make it a little easier for me?

"Do you have her address?"

"Wait a minute."

That's the kind of mother she was. She had to look up her daughter's address. Maybe that was why Suzanne was such a mess. Oh, no, I realized with a sinking feeling. My own son . . .

Ruth was back on the phone. She told me the address. I thanked her and said goodbye, but I heard the click of the phone before I finished.

She did that on purpose. Bitch! She had to

keep tissues in her panties for a weak bladder and she cleaned the wax from her ear with a hairpin. Nat had told me.

And after all I did for her daughter.

It was almost nine. I'll wait till ten and then call Steve, I decided.

I flicked on the radio. A hemorrhoid commercial. I changed the station. Soul music, husky and raucous. I couldn't understand the words. On the next station that came in, a helicopter reporter was speaking about a massive tie-up on the FDR Drive. That was a million miles away. The station after that had a supercharged, fast-talking disc jockey. Just what I didn't need for my jangled nerves. I flicked off the damned thing and went to the bathroom for a warm shower.

A hot bath brings on a period, I recalled, and changed my shower to hot and let the tub fill up. I sat in it for a few minutes. It was as hot as I could bear, but I was sure it wouldn't work. These things never did.

It would be so easy if only I started menstruating. I wouldn't have so many decisions to make or problems to solve. Steve would be angry with me if he ever found out about an abortion, but what else could I do? I wasn't young. I had a good business I had worked up from nothing.

Of course, I wouldn't want for money if I married Steve. But my business meant more than money. It meant independence. It gave me pride, an identity. Diapers and formulas and being tied down, and tying Steve down—it just wasn't for me, not now. I had enough problems with Barry.

The doorbell rang, and I let the water out of the tub.

"Coming," I called through the closed door.

It might be Barry. He might have forgotten his key. I dried myself quickly and threw on my robe.

"Who is it?" I called as I went down the steps.

"Me!"

The familiar voice made me smile. It was the first good thing that had happened to me all weekend.

Steve was standing there, holding a brown paper bag.

He kissed me on the nose and shook the bag in his hand. "Bagels. They're still hot."

"Great. I didn't eat yet."

"Barry home?"

"No." In my pleasure at seeing Steve, I had forgotten. Remembering, my expression must have changed.

"What's the matter?" he asked.

We were in the kitchen. I was filling up the teakettle while he was sitting at the table leaning forward.

First things first. "My Aunt Shirley . . ."

"The blonde bombshell?"

We both smiled. I nodded.

"Yes. She died last night."

"Oh. Sorry to hear it."

"The funeral's tomorrow. We didn't have any special plans, did we?"

Steve shook his head.

"Barry's gone," I said.

"Gone? Where?"

"I don't know. We argued early last night, and he left with Suzanne. They might be at her apartment, but I can't get in touch with them. I'm worried about him."

"He's a big boy," Steve remarked. "He can take care of himself." He took out a cigarette.

"Give me one." I lit it and inhaled. It made me dizzy. "My high for the day."

I got up to get the coffee. As I was pouring

it, Steve passed his hand over the light hairs on my arm. It was good to have him here. I bent over and kissed him on his slightly tanned, unshaven cheek. I scratched his cheek with a finger.

He smiled. "When I met you, I wasn't shaving regularly yet."

"No." I was sipping my coffee, wondering what he would think when I told him about my son. I hated to say it. It was an admission of failure, but I had to get it over with. "Steve," I began, "would you be surprised if I told you that Barry's a homosexual?"

He put down his cup and looked at me. "Is that why you two were arguing?"

"Yes. I was shocked. I *am* shocked."

"I suspected it."

"How?"

"I could tell. Men have a way of knowing. It's the way he looks at other young men. It's his friendly, nonsexual way with girls. Let's put it like this. I wondered about him."

"But you didn't tell me?"

"Why mention it? Either he is or he isn't. I don't know if you can change him."

"Do you think it was my fault?"

47

"Your fault? Silly!" he answered, but his eyes darted to my face and away quickly. That said more than words.

"You remember?"

He nodded. We knew each other well enough to communicate with a minimum of clues. We both were thinking of the time when Barry was about three.

Nat sent the baby and me to the country, to a hotel, in the summer. It was a nice hotel with a pool, a large, cool dining room, and counselors for the children. Nat came up every Friday night and left again Sunday evening.

There weren't many women my age who were there for the whole summer. The few who did come up for a week or two or a month played cards or Mah-Jongg all day. I met one girl I liked, a divorcée with two children and a rich father who picked up the bill. While she was there and flirting with the men in the band and the waiters (most of them were college or graduate students) and the occasional stray unattached male guest, it was fun for me. Her name was Laura. She was dark and pretty in a sensual way, so unlike me. We sat together at the pool and went for walks and she told me all about her ex-husband, a gambler, and her boyfriends since the divorce. Then she took up with a waiter in the nightclub, a teacher during the school year. He had days free, so I hardly saw her the last week of her vacation.

That's the way it was when a woman was looking for a man. As friendly as you got with them, you were still a temporary thing. Plans made days or weeks in advance were broken for the most casual date with a guy. I never had many girl friends, but the ones I had ran true to form. And that's how I was with them.

After Laura, I read even more than before. I was the best customer at the little library in town, for I liked classics even better than contemporary novels. Hardy depressed me and Dickens amused me, but I also suffered with the soldiers at Andersonville that summer.

On rainy days, I liked to sit in the lobby and look out of the large picture window and daydream. I was twenty-two. I had everything that money could buy and what I didn't have, I planned to get. All I had to do was nag for it or cry a few tears and Nat, dear, would get it for me.

Across from the picture window was a mirrored wall. Of course, the mirror was clouded, muting any lines or blemishes, but I enjoyed looking at myself in it although I didn't need the clouding. I was as pretty as I ever would be and prettier than I had ever been before. My hair was lighter. From ash blonde, my natural shade, I had it bleached a pale flaxen blonde. It was set every Friday night in a smart chignon. And my clothes were all of the latest fashion, expensive, perfectly matched. I had a flair for clothing. Even Laura had asked me to help her pick out clothes from the stores in town.

I knew the other women envied my youth and my looks and the men appreciated me, though, except for an occasional harmless flirtation, I ignored them. It gave me satisfaction to look well, to spend freely, to be admired. Too bad I was bored. Bored, bored, bored. Bored stiff. Stiff as a board. Bored.

When Nat came up on Friday nights, I usually had a list of complaints for him. The counselors weren't attentive enough to our son. The new women at my table in the dining room were *yentas* from Brownsville. The television set in the room had been fixed twice and still the picture jumped on channel four.

He sympathized with me, and my feelings about myself were reinforced. Surely I must be something special for him to treat me like his queen. Certainly, no one with my looks, at my age, ever made such a sacrifice for husband and child as I did staying in the hotel week after boring week. But then as well as being beautiful, I was the perfect wife and mother.

One Monday evening one of the children's waiters was fired for floating plates full of pot roast and potatoes down on the table while bombed out of his skull. He tripped and spun around and giggled as he piled filled plate upon plate. At last, we had something interesting to talk about in shocked voices all evening.

The next night I went with Barry to his dining room to cut up his food for him and urge him to eat—my main task of each day—and when I looked around to ask for more ketchup, there was the new waiter serving at the far end of the table—Steve!

We noticed each other at the same moment. He turned red and almost dropped his tray. I got busy with Barry feeling that if I were holding a tray, I, too, would fumble it.

He came to where I was sitting and, unsmiling, in fact, *angrily* asked, "What the hell are you doing here?"

My insides turned over. Immediately, I was on the defensive.

"What do you want from *me?*" I replied.

"How about my order?" someone called from another table.

He gave her a dirty look and turned back to me. "I've got to talk to you. I'm finished at eight."

He seemed so intense. I had been building up my hatred of him for three years. Just thinking how much he had hurt me made me want to hurt him back. He was bending forward, toward me, thinner than he had been, slightly tanned, his light hair striped into bands of yellow. "Will you meet me?"

"Melon," a child's voice called out. "Mommy, get me melon."

I glanced at Barry. He was mashing his vegetables. Next to me, a counselor was busy with some other children. I thought the whole room was listening to Steve, but in reality, trays were clanging, children were crying, and no one noticed us.

"Meet me at the basketball court at nine. I have to talk to you."

I didn't answer. I wanted to say no. I had daydreamed about meeting him and putting him down and here was my opportunity. Yet, in the few minutes since I'd seen him, I had felt a rush of feeling, of pure sexual excitement, that I had never felt with Nat. I had almost forgotten what it was like.

Love and hate, I thought. Twins. I had no love for Steve, just sexual attraction.

Barry was finished with his supper. He was supposed to stay with his counselor for another two hours while I dressed and then went to dinner. I left them and went to the room. I didn't want to go to the dining room, not tonight. I had too much on my mind.

I had a sandwich sent up, but I couldn't finish it. I was disturbed from seeing Steve.

The last time I saw him had been on a weekday evening, too. He was my boyfriend. At least, I thought he was. I didn't go out with anyone else hoping every day that he would surprise me with a visit and take me out, or at least call me. Most of the time, I was disappointed.

But of course, he was my boyfriend. I wouldn't let anyone except my steady boyfriend have intercourse with me whenever we saw one another. When I was menstruating, I would rub him to his climax or let him come between my breasts.

Whenever my mother was home, he'd take me out in his car and we'd park near a school yard under the black silhouette of a tree. Once a cop stopped at our car and flashed a light in at us. Steve zipped up his trousers while the policeman watched and I looked away, hot from passion and embarrassment, wishing I could melt away and disappear from the car. He asked for Steve's license and registration and told us to move on. I cried on the way home and Steve comforted me. But the next time my mother was home when Steve came to see me, we used the car again.

That last night I saw him, he called earlier in the evening to check if my house would be free. My mother was going shopping with my aunt.

I was disappointed that Steve wasn't

going to take me out, but I was anxious to see him. It was right after exams. Between his tests and his job, he had been busy. I hadn't seen him for weeks.

When he rang my doorbell and I flung open the door, I was surprised to see that he had brought a friend with him. I had never seen the boy before. He was tall and awkward with short red hair and glasses. He was too shy to look at me when we were introduced. I couldn't imagine why Steve had brought Joel with him, but I didn't have to wonder for long.

We were sitting in the living room. The tv was on. Suddenly, Steve leaned over and put his hand on my breast.

"Phyll's my girl, you know," he said to Joel. "She'd let me do anything. Right?"

I smiled. What was he leading up to?

"Joel here never made love to a girl. He doesn't think he knows how. We'll show him. OK?"

All the time he was speaking, he was rubbing my breast. His friend looked embarrassed more than anything else.

No, I wanted to tell Joel. It's not like this at all. Steve's my boyfriend.

Or was he? I looked down at his hand. In

all the months I knew him, did I really know him? Did I make him up from my imagination using the excuse of love for the thrill of sex?

"OK?" Steve repeated.

"What do you mean?" I asked.

"Come on," he urged me. He nipped at my neck. "I promised him. And I told him he could have seconds."

"What are you talking about?" I demanded. But I knew. I should have known it before. I could have, if I wanted to. Sex only. Anything else was wishful thinking on my part. God knows what he must have told Joel about me.

"Come on," he was saying. "Do me a favor."

I jumped up from the couch. My cheeks were burning. I guess I could have gone on indefinitely putting up with his broken dates and his Wednesday-night lays hoping that he'd change, but this, this new insult, was more than I would stand. I could indulge my anger. He deserved it, the lying bastard.

"Get out!"

He was surprised. "What's the matter?"

"What's the matter with *you?* What do

you think I am. I was a virgin when I met you, you bastard. Now I'm supposed to service your friends? Get out. Just go!"

They stood. Joel looked scared. He made for the door.

"You want me to go?" Steve said through tight lips, two circles of red on his cheeks. "You won't see me again."

"That's all right," I answered him. "I'm not your whore."

I slammed the door after them. They must have run to the car and left immediately, because when I looked out of the window a few minutes later, missing Steve already and hoping he'd send Joel away and come back to me, they were gone.

I didn't see Steve again. About eight months later, he called. I thrilled to his voice, but I was already engaged to be married "to my boss" as I told him when he asked. I had *that* satisfaction, at least.

I thought about him afterward, of course. I wanted to meet him again. I was rich, prettier than ever, more poised. Let him realize what a schmuck he had been.

It was almost eight-thirty. I could ask Barry's counselor to put him to bed and stay with him. Why not? Steve seemed so upset.

I would play it cool. All he wanted to do was to talk to me.

I fixed my hair and put on new makeup. First I had to speak to Barry's counselor and arrange the baby-sitting. Then, my heart pounding, I went outside to meet Steve.

The air was cool and clear. The band was practicing for the night's show and muted strains of "Eternally" drifted out over the air. The basketball court was about a city block away from the hotel. As I walked, I planned what I was going to say.

I'm a married woman, and it's a little late to be friends. I remembered. *I don't want to be your friend anyway. You betrayed me, you bastard.*

I could make out a figure on the court. For a second, the years fell away. It seemed right to be hurrying to Steve. I had to remind myself that it wasn't right at all.

Why did you bring that clown that night? Why? I was coming closer to him and forcing myself to remember. *An easy lay. That's all I was to you. An easy lay.*

I slowed up as I came nearer. Why did he have to have this effect on me? Even now as he stood there slightly hunched, thinner, older, unsmiling . . .

He stepped forward. I was in his arms

58

and, again, it seemed right, like coming home.

Remember, fool! I chided myself. I stepped out of his embrace. He leaned forward to kiss me. My body, living a life of its own, pulsated with the thought.

"No, Steve. Please. I'm a married woman."

"There are plenty of married women here. . . ."

"I said no!"

"OK." He flung up his hands. Was that a look of pain on his face or just a new trick he had learned since I saw him last? "There was something I wanted to tell you, Phyll. I made a terrible mistake to treat you the way I did," he said. "I've regretted it for years. I'm sorry."

I was glad he reminded me. Instead of getting my sympathy, as he hoped, he only reinforced my resolve. *Sorry*. It was easy enough to say.

"Let's walk," was all I answered.

We started walking down the dirt path to the lake, close but without touching. Some counselors passed us, and I turned my head away from them. Above us, the stars looked as though they had just been scrubbed with ammonia.

"I wanted to say it to you. I knew I would get to say it someday, but I didn't know when or where. I'm sorry, Phyll."

Sure. Sure. He found himself a new line, I thought. We were at the lake. Flying things made little pings of noise as they landed on the water.

He stepped closer. "I've been trying to figure it out, Phyll. I think I wasn't ready then. I was eighteen. I thought I knew it all, but I was dumb. I didn't know anything." He stopped as though waiting for me to say something. I waited. "I loved you and I didn't know it."

He put his face to mine and kissed me very gently on the lips. When I felt his tongue, I moved my face away.

"No," I said. "Everything's different now. I have a husband. I have a child. I've had to mature."

"But—"

"You can't wish the years away. *I* can't. Come on. Let's walk back. Tell me. Are you finished with your schooling now?"

We walked back along the path and he told me he was going into his final year of law school. I asked him about his life since I last saw him, but he kept returning like music to the same theme. *I never had another serious girlfriend after you. I was stupid. Crazy. Forgive me. Trust me.*

When I left him, without another kiss, he asked me to meet him again the next night.

I told him the truth. "I don't know."

I wanted him. But I wasn't going to fall into bed with him at the snap of his fingers. Fall into bed. I had been faithful to Nat all the years of our marriage. Nat's a good guy, I thought. But I'm young. I'm entitled to some excitement. In my room, I put on my nightgown and made my bed thinking that I'd be staying up the rest of the night worrying about Steve and me. The walk must have tired me. Within seconds, I was fast asleep. I hadn't slept so well for weeks.

When I awoke the next morning, Barry was sleeping in my bed, warm and moist beside me. He must have learned how to climb out of his crib.

I thought of Steve. If I were sincere, I'd tell Nat I want to go home with him when he comes up to see us on the weekend. I could do that. I should. But I wouldn't.

That evening after dinner, I sat in a remote corner of the lobby talking to Steve.

The windows, dotted with raindrops, seemed to insulate us from the outside. Two of the women from my table in the dining room noticed us there and, embarrassed, stopped to chat with me as though they expected to find me sitting there with a handsome man my own age.

"This is Steve," I introduced him. "He's an old friend of mine. Coincidentally, he's my son's waiter."

"Isn't that something!" the livelier of the two women remarked. But I knew that when they were five feet away from us they'd begin their gossiping.

"How can I see you? Can I come to your room?" Steve asked later.

"You can come up, Steve, if you want to talk."

He looked hurt.

"I'm serious. Nothing else."

"OK. I'll go by your rules."

I went up to the room first and paid the baby-sitter. Then Steve came in. Barry was asleep in his crib, but I had set up a screen between Barry and my side of the room anyway.

This time, Steve had his hands all over me. We wrestled, clothed, on the bed. I let him push me down, but when I felt his hand on the zipper of my slacks, I sprang up.

"Please, Steve."

He sat up, obviously angry.

Good, I thought. I stopped him. Serves him right. "My husband's coming tomorrow night. I'll see you again on Monday night."

"I don't give a damn about your husband," he answered.

"I know you don't. But I do." I was getting angry at myself. Who the hell was he to dismiss Nat like that! What did he think I was—the same easy lay I had been? "You come back into my life after four years, and you think things haven't changed?"

"Have they?" He was standing now, adjusting his jeans.

The way the room was arranged, there was a mirror almost everywhere you looked. It was disconcerting to turn your back on one mirror and again come face to face with yourself.

Steve lowered his voice. "I went to a shrink for about a year. I wanted to know why I acted the way I did with you." He looked away, as though he were embarrassed. I had never seen him like this before.

"Why did you?"

"My whole outlook was distorted. I thought since you were easy for me, it would be easy to replace you. I never have."

Again, my reaction wavered between belief and distrust. No matter how he justified himself, I would never forgive him.

Barry stirred in his sleep. He called out something I couldn't understand. I waited for him to get quiet, and then I turned again to Steve.

"I thought you were out of my system. Until I saw you. You know," he said sitting on the edge of my bed, "I haven't even talked to another girl like I talked to you yesterday and today. You've got to give me another chance."

"Let me think, Steve," I answered. "Till after the weekend. Let's wait till then."

I want him, I thought as he kissed me a quick good-bye, not because I felt sorry for him or believed what he said, although he could think what he wished. I wanted him as he had once wanted me. Love had nothing to do with it.

I was in a bad mood by the time Nat came up on Friday night. Even before I saw him in the lobby, I heard his loud accented voice joking with some men about playing cards that night.

Barry ran to him and I followed, slowly, conscious of my lack of feeling.

There he was—my husband; smiling, lines radiating from his eyes, his face covered with black stubble (he had to shave twice a day). He was wearing an iridescent shirt I had picked out for him. It was much too youthful, I realized as I watched him.

He hugged Barry and chortled when he saw me. "That's my wife," he said to the other men when I reached him. They were strangers to me. He kissed me, smelling of cigar smoke and put a finger under my chin to show my face to his friends.

"What do you think of her?"

"Oh, Nat, really!" I laughed. He treated me as if I were his teenage daughter.

Nat made his date for poker and I told him to take Barry to dinner while I changed. Last week, we had both gone with our son while he ate. But now that wouldn't do at all. I smiled to myself. Not at all.

I wondered what Steve would think of Nat. He was nothing to look at. Short, only a few inches taller than me, with a potbelly, and hair partly gray, he looked older than forty. He hadn't been bad looking in his youth—I had seen pictures—but he was never anything like Steve. And he was nervous. He spoke rapidly, walked too quickly, forgot what he was saying, cursed mechanical things, was sloppy. He was good at making money, and he was generous with it. I'll say that for him.

I put Barry to sleep myself that evening for the first time in three nights. Nat was playing cards He didn't want to go to the show in the nightclub. I had hired a sitter. And though I really didn't care about going, it was a good reason to get peeved at Nat. I went back to the room to read.

When Nat came in, at about one in the morning, he apologized. "I'm going to take a shower," he announced meaningfully.

I yawned. "I'm exhausted from waiting for you," I told him. "Don't wake me up if I fall asleep."

Of course, I was fast asleep by the time he came back to bed.

I got up with Barry the next morning and took him down to breakfast. I was the first parent there.

"I saw your husband," Steve told me.

He stood over me and Barry without speaking for a long few seconds.

"I married him on the rebound, you know."

He nodded somberly and walked away.

Now why in the world did I say that? I thought. I didn't have to apologize for Nat, least of all to Steve.

When Barry's counselor came in, I bolted out of the dining room. I wanted to think.

My mother had been glad I married Nat. Nat had friends who thought I was a very lucky young girl. So what if he was so much older and a foreigner with only a little education. He was rich. He was kind. And he was the father of my darling little boy, the best thing that ever happened to me.

If I were going to be unfaithful to him, well, I didn't mean anything personally. Nat was all right. He couldn't help being dull and ugly, and I was damned if I'd go back to the room though I knew he was expecting me.

I'll buy a newspaper, I decided, and sit in the lobby and read it. When he comes down, for breakfast, I'll pretend I just left Barry.

I managed to avoid Nat until that evening. I came out of the shower, thinking

I was alone, and there was Nat in his pajamas.

"Where's Barry?"

"He finished eating. He's with his group." He beckoned me to the bed. "Come on now. I haven't been with you in the room all weekend."

"We'll be late for dinner."

"We won't be late. Don't worry. Come to bed."

I hesitated. Last weekend I was menstruating. I couldn't keep putting him off. Reluctantly, I started to the bed.

"Wait. Let me look at you first."

Let him look at me? It was bad enough I had to let him screw me. I didn't have to perform for him, too!

"You wearing something?" I asked, referring to birth control.

"Yes."

He started to pet me, but I wanted to be finished quickly.

"That's all right," I told him. "You come on top."

In a few minutes—neither particularly exciting nor revolting—he came to his climax and it was over. I had done my wifely duty. Feeling so little, I could be objective. I could make my choice. Was there a choice?

On Sunday, while we were sitting by the pool, Nat asked me, "Do you like it here? Are you enjoying yourself? Did you make any friends?"

His words came out in a barrage. At one time, it had unnerved me, but by now I was used to it. I selected one of his questions to answer.

"It's all right."

"You ought to learn how to play cards or Mah-Jongg," he continued. "Sam's wife seems like a nice girl. You could be friendly with her. Do you have any friends here?"

For a second, I played with the idea of telling him about Steve. No. I couldn't.

"I don't like to play cards," I answered. "And the women are all much older than me."

"Oh."

That shut him up. I knew his weak points. Age was one of them.

I lay back on the lounge and let the sun soak into me.

"How about some poker?"

I sat up. Two of Nat's cronies were

standing at the foot of our lounges.

"I have to ask the wife," Nat answered them. "You mind if I play?"

"No. That's all right. It's almost lunchtime, anyway. I want to check on—Barry." I almost said *Steve*. Now that would have been a clever thing to say.

Nat beamed. "What a girl! Isn't she something?" He threw his arms around me and kissed me wetly on the cheek. "She's some kid."

I waited until he had gone off with his friends and they were out of sight before I wiped my cheek.

When it was a little after twelve, I went to the children's dining room where Barry was eating. Steve was there, but we didn't get a chance to speak.

Nat left for the city at about five. Barry was napping, and I stayed in the room with him until it was time to awaken him for supper. I had showered and fixed my hair, my cheeks red from the sun and from anticipation.

I couldn't eat in the main dining room with that table full of harpies. They'd certainly ask why I wasn't going to Bingo tonight, and since some of them had already seen Steve with me, it was obvious that I'd choose him over a silly game.

"I'll eat here with my son," I told Barry's waiter, but when the food came, I picked at it, too excited to eat.

Steve came over once. He was on the verge of speaking, but the room suddenly got quiet and all I could do was greet him. I told Barry's counselor to bring him up to the room after the evening session and put him to bed. Then I sat in the lobby and waited.

Oh, damn it. Those two women from my table were coming my way. I turned my face away, hoping they wouldn't notice me.

"Phyllis. Why are you sitting here alone?"

I forced a smile. "I'm just resting."

She leaned closer, smelling of talcum powder. "Nat told us he thought you weren't having a good time," she went on. "He told us to take you under our wing."

At three hundred pounds, she had plenty of wing, I thought. She was grotesquely fat. Leave it to Nat to pair me with her.

I smiled.

"Aren't you going to go to dinner?" the thinner one asked. She would only be thinner in the Catskills. She was no light-weight either. "It's after eight."

"No. I wasn't hungry. I had a bite to eat in the children's dining room."

I noticed Steve out of the corner of my eye. He was at the other end of the lobby. He must see us, I thought.

"How did you like last night's show?"

The fat one sat, and then the other, on either side of me. I felt trapped.

"I missed it. You'll be late for dinner," I blurted out to the heavier one.

"I can wait. Did you eat the sundae for dessert at lunch?"

"No." I was never going to get rid of them.

"Oh," the thinner one picked up for her friend, "was it scrumptious. Coffee ice cream with bits of chocolate and a coffee-flavored sauce."

That gave me an idea. "Oh," I moaned. I slapped a hand on my chest. "You'll have to excuse me. Something I ate for supper doesn't agree with me. I need some Pepto Bismol."

"I have some in my room," one of the women volunteered.

They *were* nice. Not as nice as Steve

would be. . . .

"Thanks, but I have some upstairs, too. Enjoy your dinner."

I went to the elevator hoping that Steve was watching. I couldn't turn around as I was sure the women were still looking my way. I stepped into the elevator when it opened, and as I faced outward and pushed the button, Steve hurried into it, just making it as the doors began to close.

"I thought I'd never get away," I told him.

He kissed me quickly on the lips. The elevator stopped. A honeymoon couple I had noticed checking in a few minutes before stepped into the elevator. The girl was wearing a white corsage that was turning brown around the edges.

She smiled to us. I smiled back.

"Are you here long?" the girl asked. Her gesture took in Steve, me, and the rest of the hotel.

"Yes," I replied, a little too eagerly.

I looked away from her to the numbers blinking over the doors. Finally, the elevator stopped and Steve and I got out.

We walked without speaking until the doors of the elevator were shut.

He was shaking his head slowly. "You're really lousy at this," he said. "Guilt is written all over your face."

"Why do you have to tell me that?"

Somewhere behind one of the doors, a baby was crying.

"When will your son be back?" Steve asked.

"He's in the room now. We can't go there."

He stopped short. "Why did we use the elevator then?"

"I didn't know what to do. I wanted to get away from those women."

"We'll go to my place. No one's there."

"We can't go through the lobby again," I reminded him.

"Come on." He grabbed me by the wrist. "We'll use the stairs."

We went out on the back steps of the emergency exit. In the parking lot below us, a man was loading a valise into the trunk of his car. I recognized him.

"We can't go down now," I told Steve. "That's Nat's friend."

We stepped back into the hallway. Barry's baby-sitter could come into the hall and catch us there. This was crazy.

"Why'd you have to tell me I'm lousy at cheating on my husband? Why'd you have to make me feel guiltier?" I whispered.

Steve's face softened. He touched my cheek with his finger. "Let's be honest with one another. This isn't the way I want it, either."

No? I thought. It seemed that this way he could have what he wanted—me, his old lay—without any permanent attachment. But I didn't say anything. I wasn't any better than he was.

The baby was still crying behind a door. I wondered if his mother was with him.

Steve opened the fire door again and looked out. "Come on," he told me over his shoulder. "The coast is clear."

I followed him, letting him walk ahead of me while we were passing the entrance to the hotel. When we were at the door to his cabin, he told me to wait. He opened the door and flicked on the light.

"OK. Come in."

The cabin smelled from dampness and mold. Two beds, both unmade, with gray sheets dangling loosely, filled most of the room. There were also a couple of dressers, obvious castoffs from the main building, leaning like drunks against the wall, their drawers opened haphazardly, the wood on them peeled and broken.

Calendar pictures of nude girls were taped to the walls behind the beds and were reflected in the speckled mirror opposite. A sink was in the room. It was striped with wide orange lines where the faucets dripped. Overhead, rusty pipes were exposed.

"Well," Steve remarked, "it's nothing fancy."

The absurdity of the situation got to me. I exploded into a fit of laughter. Steve, too. He held me and we laughed hysterically. Tears rolled down our cheeks and we had to bend to relieve the ache in our sides.

"It's awful, isn't it?" Steve asked when we finally stopped.

I nodded.

"I'm sorry," he whispered into my hair.

"Where can we go?"

"I'll ask at the desk. Maybe there's a room available in the hotel."

"OK."

Neither of us moved. I wished I weren't so fussy. It was enough of an ordeal getting here.

"Bugs, too, I guess?" I asked him.

"Yeah."

That settled it. His place wasn't going to be it. I looked around. "You don't have a phone here?"

"No. You'll have to go up to your room and I'll ask at the front desk."

I thought of the women I was trying to avoid. They'd probably be in the lobby now. I didn't want Steve to be so obvious. I shook my head. "I'd rather you didn't go to the desk unless you're sure they have a room. Call them from one of the other phones on the corner of the lobby."

"OK."

Outside the cabin, the air smelled of grass and, faintly, insecticide.

I waited for Steve to turn out the light and close the door.

"Sunburns and dirty cabins," I reminded him as we started back to the hotel. "We don't have great beginnings."

"They're great," he murmured. "And it's going to be greater. Go on," he told me as we neared the entrance. "I'll follow you in. Wait for my call."

A quick hug and I was hurrying back to the lights and the noise and the people, wondering about Steve. He seemed so mature, so kind. But you could never tell till afterward, I reminded myself. What if he's sincere? I thought. I'd have to worry about that later.

When I got back to my room, Barry was sleeping and his baby-sitter was watching television.

"I might go out again," I told her when she got up to leave. "I'm waiting for a phone call. I'll get it when it rings," I added—unnecessarily, I realized as soon as I said it.

A few minutes later, the phone rang.

"There are no rooms."

This was our last alternative. After my room, there was nothing left but the grass.

"I'll let my baby-sitter go."

"Will ten minutes be enough time?"

"Yes."

"Then I'll be up in ten minutes. Wait for me."

I smiled. I wanted to say, I'm not planning on going anywhere, but the baby-sitter was still there, listening.

I paid the girl and set up the screen between Barry's bed and mine. It was the wrong time, the wrong place, the wrong person, but I never once thought of stopping. Not once during all our ridiculously complicated arrangements. When Steve came up, I put out the light and we undressed in the dark. It was oddly exciting taking off my clothes to the sound of my son's even breathing.

Steve held me tenderly, actually more gentle than he had ever been before with me. He took me, and it was good then. It was good after, too, with him lying next to me, leaning over to kiss my shoulder or stroke my cheek. Maybe he had been telling the truth. Maybe he did miss me.

You have to go, I thought. Barry might wake up though he rarely awakened once he was asleep, but I was too weary to say anything. I must have dozed for a few minutes. When I opened my eyes again, Steve was dressed.

"I'm going," he whispered, "but I'll see you tomorrow. Say I'm your friend from high school so I can talk to you."

"I don't know," I answered. "I think it looks suspicious. And the women are such gossip mongers."

"Damn it, Phyll." He sat down hard on the bed. "What the hell are you protecting? I told you I love you. The minute you break up with your husband . . ."

His voice had been getting louder. My hand tightened on his arm.

His voice dropped again. "You don't believe me, do you? Believe me, Phyll. Trust me."

The next morning Barry woke up bubbling with a cold and hot with fever. I had his cereal sent up, but he didn't want it. I gave him aspirin and put on the hot water in the shower for steam and had my meals sent up to the room, nursing and sponging and amusing my son patiently partly out of guilt, no doubt, but mostly because he was my beautiful little baby, and he was sick.

When Steve called, I told him to call again in the evening. I didn't want him in the room with me while Barry was awake. I spent a long, boring day alone with the baby, but in the evening Barry's temperature was lower and his cold was a little better, though he still had some discomfort in breathing.

He fell asleep right after his supper, and when Steve called, I told him to come up. A few minutes later, he was at the door holding a paper bag.

"I heard this was a bottle party," he

joked, showing me the bottle of champagne he had brought. "I thought it would cheer you up," he explained.

We drank it from the glasses in the bathroom and when we finished, I flicked off the lights.

We took longer this time. He was more playful, more sure of himself. It was the joyous experience it always was with him. How funny that I had spent years in remorse for having been so easy for him, but since last night, I had forgiven myself completely. This was the way it should be. All those years in between, I was thinking with my head not with a body that tingled to his touch.

We lay in each other's arms afterward. It was still early, but we both drifted into a deep sleep. I was awakened by Steve sitting up abruptly. Hot liquid touched the side of my face.

"Barry!" Steve exclaimed.

"Barry!" I repeated.

There was Barry standing next to our bed, his pajamas around his feet, calmly urinating on Steve.

"Get back to your crib," I screamed at him. He walked away, his pajamas still around his feet.

Steve and I were naked. I felt in the bed and on the floor for my nightgown and put it on. I got Steve his pants.

"I'm terribly sorry," I apologized.

"It's a first for me," Steve replied, a hint of a laugh in his voice. "I dreamed it was raining. I'm going in for a quick shower."

While he was in the bathroom, I sat on the edge of the bed wondering what I was going to do about Barry. I didn't know.

Steve came out in a few minutes and kissed me good night, promising to call in the morning.

I latched the door and went to Barry. His forehead was hot.

"Who that man, Mommy? Who that?"

"Shush," I told him going for aspirin and water. When I came back to his crib, he asked again, "Who that man?"

He took his aspirin and I thought of an answer.

"What man?" I replied. "You had a dream. Silly. You had a silly dream." He didn't ask me again.

And now the man of the dream, some fourteen years later, put his hand over mine. I held it. Guilt engulfed me like a wave. I was so young then and passionate, and I thought I was so clever covering up for myself. Who knows what damage I did to my son?

"What will you do when Barry comes home?" Steve asked me.

"I don't know." I had to decide on something. "The whole problem overwhelms me," I muttered.

"It's better he's away then. You have to accept him the way he is. *Any* way."

"It's easy for you to say," I retorted.

Steve raised his eyebrow. I shouldn't have said that, I realized. Steve was concerned. He wanted to help. I stood up and went to him. To apologize. To make up.

Later in bed after I came to an orgasm, he pushed me down on him. He knew I didn't like oral sex. I never did it with anyone else. Never with Nat.

Now I had a new thought. Is this what Barry does? What could he see in it? It tasted salty. Further down, it felt like tiny wires the size of hairpins, on rubber. Steve liked it best, but when he started to come and that warm slime shot out of him, it was disgusting. I choked on it. How could Barry?

We washed and went back to bed. It was pleasant lying there curled up against Steve as he sat on the edge of the bed lighting a cigarette.

"Your son should have had a father."

For a second I was startled. How did he know? No. He didn't know I was pregnant. He was still talking about Barry.

"It's not too late," he added.

I cuddled up against him warm and snug. He had asked me before. He had wanted to marry me after Nat's death, but I was frightened of marriage.

For a while, it seemed that almost every couple we knew was separating or divorcing. And it wasn't easy after a long marriage. My neighbor walked around like a zombie, her eyes red and swollen. Her son dropped out of school in a state of depression. All because her short, overweight forty-five-year-old husband found himself a twenty-year-old girl he wanted to live with.

"Believe me, add up all the good times and it's not worth this hell," she told me the last time I had seen her. She was still waiting for him to come back.

And the good marriages, the ones that stuck, always seemed based on a weakness of one of the partners. Sometimes it was based on a total dependence of the wife on the husband for one thing—like money— while the husband had no friends, no social contact, no ability to enjoy anything other than his work, without his wife. The two of them would have made one complete well-adjusted individual, but as a couple each of them remained a half person.

Dependence and deception. That's what my marriage to Nat had been. I didn't want *that* again.

What I had with Steve seemed perfect. We were together, yet we were free. He had his own apartment, but he'd stay at my house for days at a time. When we argued or got on one another's nerves, we separated. The door was always open for his return. I dreaded the thought that he might leave me; it would be easy for him *not* to return, but that was the price of freedom.

Once during one of our periods of separation, Steve married. He told me about it over the phone.

"I want a family, Phyll," he explained.

"And she's a wonderful girl."

While he told me about all her wonderful qualities on that hot June day, the walls melted, the floors buckled, and I could hardly hear what he was saying above the screech that suddenly whistled in the telephone wires.

"Would you like to come to the wedding?" he asked me.

He was too much, my ex-lover. "No. No, thank you."

"You're not mad at me?"

"I could never be mad at you, Steve." I choked out false good wishes and hung up the phone.

Fool! Fool! I told myself. I let him go once too often.

"What's the matter?" Barry was home reading a sports book.

"Nothing. Nothing,"
I cried, choked and sobbing. It was harder for me losing Steve that way than losing Nat the other way.

The marriage lasted four months. He came to see me after he got back from his honeymoon. He was chain-smoking. There were lines around his eyes I never noticed before. He sat slumped and weary on a kitchen chair and told me about her.

"She's spoiled. Spoiled and childish. She doesn't know how to relate to another person." He rubbed his eyes with the fingers of one hand. "She was a virgin. I'll say that for her."

My laugh was bitter. He got her virginity, or at least he thought he did. Now he wanted to get rid of his child bride.

He drank what I handed him in one gulp. His fingers on my skin were cold.

"No, no," I told him. "I don't want you to be unfaithful." What was I saying? Clearly, I wanted to show him that his bride wasn't the only one with morals. He was gentleman enough to insist.

Afterward, I realized how much we had to rebuild. He should have laughed at my protests. I should have laughed at his predicament. They were both absurd.

I couldn't laugh then. While he was dressing, I broke down.

"Come back," I begged him. "We'll get married if you want. Or if you don't want to, we won't. Whatever you want. Only come back, Steve."

I would have married him, gladly, after his divorce, but then he was leery of marriage. Slowly, through the years, he told me about his ex-wife.

They had gone to Mexico for their honeymoon. On the third night there, he came done with cramps and vomiting. She was disgusted with him.

"I didn't come to Mexico to sit in the room listening to you being sick," she told him.

"Go downstairs if you want," he answered her, feeling too lousy to give a damn. But when she took out a gown to put on, he lifted his head from the pillow.

"Where are you going?"

"To the nightclub. You don't think I'm going to sit in the lobby with the old people."

When he was better, he told her how I had come to his apartment one time when he had the virus, making some lame excuse to Nat, so that I could boil tea for him and give him his medicine.

"Maybe you should have married Phyllis," was her reply.

"Maybe you're right," was his.

She had agreed that they would have a family right away. Steve was thirty and anxious to have a child.

"She quit her job," he told me, "and since

she didn't like doing housework, we hired a maid. She also didn't like to cook, so we ate out most of the time. I didn't care. I wanted her to rest and be happy and be ready to conceive. There I was plugging away and nothing happened. I was beginning to get worried. I made an appointment for us with a doctor.

"Then one day I happened to be looking for a stamp, and what do I find in her night table but a diaphragm and a tube of spermicide. She used to put it on before I came home from work. What hurt me was that she never saw fit to discuss it with me. I would have waited if she wanted to have a baby later on. I wanted the marriage to work. But I saw it was hopeless."

He came back to me after he left her, bowed and saddened. Whoever she was, she wasn't worth it—the bitch!

He didn't want marriage again then, but he was more devoted than ever. Before his marriage, he used to occasionally go out with other women. He gave that up. Recently, he started speaking of getting married again.

Was that how I conceived? I wondered. Did he slip it past me? It was possible, even probable. I wouldn't know unless I asked him, and once I asked him everything would be changed.

I put my arms around his waist (getting flabby) and he turned so that I could put my head on his chest where the hair was like delicate rings of silver and gold.

He was waiting for me to speak. I answered him the only way I could. "I love you, Steve." I was sure of that, at least.

I had an appointment with some customers in the afternoon. I left a note for Barry in case he returned while both Steve and I were out, though I doubted he'd return so quickly.

I kissed Steve good-bye, and I went to pick up the customers. They were a youngish couple I had been taking shopping for a few years. That was how long it was taking them to furnish their home. Today they were going to look for a dining-room set.

"You know me, Mrs. Albert," the husband liked to say. "I don't need fancy furniture, I can eat off a wooden crate."

It was his standard speech, and I playfully winked at his wife. "He tells us that every time, right? But I noticed who looked very comfortable on the new sofa."

His wife shook her head. Part of the skit we reenacted every time I took them buying was her playful annoyance with him.

"And who puts his glass with a wet bottom on the end tables?" she replied. "Maybe he would be better off on an orange crate."

We laughed, and they continued with their gentle teasing. They seemed happy with one another, at least at this time in their lives. What would happen if the roles they played began to irk them? Or one of them changed? Or they got bored or angry or resentful?

Even without seeing Steve every day, I could guess what was on his mind from his expression, what his answers would be, what stories would remind him of particular events in the past. I didn't want to know him so well that I'd be bored with him as I had been bored with Nat. I used to feel like screaming when he began one of his repetitious stories or he grinned foolishly and demanded, "Look at my wife, will you?" I couldn't stand his habits: dipping cake into coffee, cutting orange rinds into tiny pieces, brushing crumbs on a table to the floor. At his funeral, the thought suddenly occurred to me, I'll never have to clean out his curly pubic hairs from the drain when I take my shower.

I guess you can get to hate a person from the way he squeezes the toothpaste tube. Was there a chance for any marriage?

And yet when we were driving home from the showroom and the Greenes were chatting happily about the set they had just put a deposit on, it seemed good to be mated.

"Wasn't it something the way Bernie picked out the set just as I was going to point it out?" his wife said.

"I like the fabric you two decided on. It should really show up good in the dining room," he answered her.

Pleased with one another, and their happiness was catching. I hoped Steve would be home when I returned. He was. He had gone to see a client and come back, he told me. My mother had called. She was going to the funeral chapel in the evening, and she wanted to know if we were going.

I sank into a chair in the living room aware suddenly that my feet were aching. I should go to see if my period had started, I thought, but I didn't feel like getting up.

"I told your mother we'll pick her up at eight."

"Thanks, Steve." Taking my mother to the chapel was one of the acts of kindness I appreciated him for. I got up and went to sit next to him on the couch, resting my head on his shoulder.

He put a big, bony hand on my arm. I blew on the light fuzz that covered it. The smell of cigarette smoke clung to the shirt he was wearing.

"You look tired," he remarked. "Want to rest for a while?"

"No." I sat up straighter. I didn't want him to guess why I looked tired. Poor Steve. I was being unfair to him. If only I knew my own mind. "I'm all right," I told him.

"Let's go out to eat. I'm getting hungry," he said.

"OK. I just want to wash up and change."

I wrote a new note to Barry when we were ready to go, telling him where we would be. Steve read it over my shoulder.

"Why do you sign it 'Mother'?"

"What should I write?"

"How about 'Love, Mother.'"

I considered it. "No. I can't. I'm mad at him."

"Mad at him? He's not a baby, Phyll. He'll stay away if you don't show him respect."

"Respect? How can I respect him when he's—you know." I went into the other room to turn off the lights, leaving one light on to confuse any thieves. "When I think of him with another boy . . ."

"Then don't think of him with another boy!" Steve sounded angry. "You know, every day I deal with families where people can't accept one another. Phyll, you're the parent. You have to lead him."

"Don't they need psychiatry?"

"I don't know. I guess some try to change, and others learn to live with it."

I was back in the room with the note. I put it in a more prominent place on the counter, but I still didn't add the word.

"I'd feel like a hypocrite writing *Love*. It's like saying, I accept you. Go find yourself a nice boy and live happily ever after. I can't."

"Sex is only a part of life. It's not the whole show."

"No?"

We were at the door. Steve was getting a light jacket from the closet. "Want a jacket?" I shook my head. I was warm enough. Too warm, most of the time.

I didn't always agree with him, but he had a way of calming me. If it were Nat, running and stuttering in that fast, jerky manner, I'd be out of my mind by now. If it were any of a hundred men . . .

He leaned forward and kissed me on the forehead. "Don't worry about him," he murmured. "He's a good kid."

Steve, I thought, you were right. Barry should have had you as a father. I wish I weren't so goddamned frightened.

Saturday Night

My mother was waiting in front of her apartment house when we came to get her. Her eyes were red from crying. When she saw us, they filled up again.

"Isn't it terrible?" she said. "Sixty years old was all she was." She wiped her face with a tissue and maneuvered herself slowly into the back seat. When she was settled, she threw a kiss to Steve. "How are you, Steve?"

"I'm all right, thanks. And you?"

"Well, you know. It was a shock. I was thinking, my sister died early, but she had a good life."

She opened her fist. There was a crumpled ball of tissues in it, and she studied it with surprise.

"Look what I did while I was waiting for you. Do *you* have tissues?"

Before I could answer, she continued. "You should have taken a sweater. Those places are always freezing. Do you have one?"

I shook my head. "No."

She clucked in annoyance.

Steve smiled. It amused him when she treated me like a child. I put up with it. It was easier than arguing with her.

"I spoke to Moe," my mother began again. "He sounded strong, like he was talking about the death of an acquaintance. Well, he was good to her." (*Too* good, she used to say.) "Steve, you met Moe?"

Steve nodded. They had met on perhaps

fifteen occasions. Each time they were reintroduced to one another.

"You know, he's rich as Croesus. My daughter should be so rich."

Now what did she mean by that? I wondered. I glanced at her.

"I don't mean anything bad by that," she said, peeved. "You know, my sister had some life. Some life." Her voice became husky for the moment. Then it returned to normal. "Started out fast. That's how she got him."

Here we go again.

"Her *third* husband. She shopped and shopped and went back to return, and finally she got one she decided to keep." She stopped and I looked back at her. She was wiping her eyes. Shirley had been her junior by three years. My mother, the fat, ungainly, unlucky one, had outlived her beautiful sister. Was she really heartbroken?

We drove up to the funeral home and Steve stopped the car to let her out. She tugged at the handle.

"I can never open the door to this car," she said.

I leaned over and opened it for her. She

got out. I watched her waddle away with mixed feelings. She was my mother and I loved her, but spending even a few hours in her company could reduce me to the emotional level of a child.

I stayed with Steve while he parked. My cousin, Jack, pulled into the lot as we were walking away, and we waited for him.

Though it was his mother who had died, he shook Steve's hand like the greeter at a convention and planted a wet, noisy kiss on my lips. His voice, too, bubbly and booming, was inappropriately hearty.

"You're looking terrific, Cuz," he told me. "Taking care of her, Steve? No kidding, how are you?" (This, to Steve.)

"I'm fine. Sorry to hear about your mother."

"Yes." Jack shook his head once. "Well, the doctors couldn't help her past a point. We knew it was coming."

Jack had grown fat. I noted with dismay his huge beer belly, probably the result of living a bachelor's life with no one really to care for him. Twice divorced, I didn't think he wanted to remarry.

He had been skinny once and good-looking. "The handsomest boy in the navy,"

Aunt Shirley had called him, proudly displaying his picture. He must have been eighteen at the time, and I agreed with Aunt Shirley. He *was* the handsomest boy, and I had a crush on him.

(We used to jump rope spelling out the name of the boy we loved. Loved? We were seven and eight and nine, and I remember my friend asking me, *Who's Jack?)*

Jack was opening the door to the chapel, his voice echoing in the hushed surroundings. "Cy was going to arrange for her to come to New York to the hospital, but her doctor in Florida told him not to move her. And the next thing . . ."

Moe came out of a room into the hall with my mother. The skin of his round apple face hung looser around his pink little mouth than I remembered.

"Do you know Steve? Phyllis' friend?" my mother asked him.

"Yes. I know Steve. How are you, kids?"

Kids. Everything is relative. I kissed him and murmured our sympathy and we went back with him into the room off the lobby to speak about his wife.

"Better this way," he said, wiping his face with a handkerchief. It was a big white cloth handkerchief, the kind my father used to use. I hadn't seen one like it for years. "She wasn't herself when she was sick. And she *was* something. The life of the party. Wherever she went, people loved her. Strangers."

My mother sat there dabbing at her eyes, but those eyes flashed denial and her lips were tightly shut.

"Such a kind heart," Moe was going on. He turned to my mother, flinging out his hands. "Well, you know."

The look my mother gave him was one of pure hatred. But I was the only one there who could read it. "Why shouldn't she give?" my mother used to say after Shirley had come by with a box of clothing for her or for me. "I'm her only sister. Phyllis is her only niece. Clothing. Big deal. For a woman who sparkles with jewelry and has more fur than a zoo keeper, it's the least she could do!"

To Shirley's face, she was grateful. How I hated to watch my mother humble herself with her sister especially when she prided herself on being outspoken and honest. For a long time, I remember, I was confused.

Suddenly while I was sitting there listen-

104

ing to Moe talk, I realized that my earliest memory involved Aunt Shirley. Back, back in time, I recalled my mother with her brown eyes sparkling in anger, her lips a thin pink line. Her look of anger was directed toward my father.

It was still the Depression. Years later, the history books would say that the hard times were ending by then, but on the fall day I remember, my father still didn't have a job. My mother worked part-time in a dry goods store—she hated it—and only Aunt Shirley was rich.

I had heard about it so many times that I had a clear picture of the event. Aunt Shirley had roped herself a third husband. I pictured Uncle Moe, flat-nosed and pie-faced, with a rope like a belt around his waist. The end of the rope was in the silk-gloved hand of Aunt Shirley.

Aunt Shirley. No matter what my mother said, I adored my aunt with her curly blonde hair and her face like a doll's. She even smelled pretty. Like a flower. And when she sat on our couch (she was company) and opened a compact because her nose was shiny (now why was that so bad?), I watched the delicate fingers that held the powder puff; her nails were petals, and I marveled that those were the same fingers that she used to rope her husband.

The day they visited I was dressed in a dotted-swiss red pinafore, Aunt Shirley's latest gift to me. The pillows on the sofa were puffed up until they were as round as Uncle Moe's cheeks, and on every arm of furniture our lace antimacassars were placed in perfect symmetry. I was warned not to touch.

In the kitchen, my mother, as usual, was telling my father what he should do. "Tell them we won't live in no basement apartment. But be polite. If he has a nice apartment—two bedrooms—and some small payment—thirty-five dollars a week to start—that would be all right."

My father listened in silence. He was a big, handsome bear of a man. When he spoke it was with a husky voice and an inappropriate stutter. He moved as he spoke—hesitantly, as though afraid to jostle the little people around him. It must have been a comical sight—the round, fat little shrew of a woman ordering her big stuttering husband around—but, of course,

I didn't find it funny.

Finally, they came. The twins, Cy and Jackie, rushed in like a burst of wind. The antimacassars slid to the floor as they jumped on the couch making deep circles in the pillows.

"Go downstairs and play. And don't get dirty."

Aunt Shirley had a gift for me. A beautiful glass tea set. Flowers more perfect than on any bush blossomed in the middle of every plate and cup. I wanted to stay and play with it, but I was sent downstairs after my cousins.

"Watch Phyllis," Aunt Shirley called to the boys, from the window.

The boys were playing stoopball.

"Sit on the bench," Cy told me. "And if you move I'll break every bone in your body."

I sat and watched them play. After a long time, my mother leaned out the window. "Come on up for supper."

We went up and ate. Afterward, the adults played cards till late. Jackie fell asleep and had to be awakened for the trip home. He stood leaning against Moe, still half asleep, while Cy watched the good-byes through heavy lids. I had napped early in the day and I wasn't as tired as my cousins.

There was a great deal of laughing and kissing and then my mother said to me, "Come. Give your Uncle Moe a great big kiss. He's giving your father an important job in a beautiful apartment house he owns."

"But, Mommy," (and now I'm not sure if I've been told it so many times that I think I remember it or if it is my actual memory) "I thought Uncle Moe owns horses."

Uncle Moe's cheeks lifted in a smile. "Horses? What ever gave you that idea?"

"Mommy said you got one of the biggest *horse* in Brooklyn."

My mother was the first to realize what I said. She might have covered up for me, but Moe caught on before she could say anything, and his face turned a beet red. Aunt Shirley was smiling from the general pleasantness of the situation. The smile remained pasted on her lips. Then as she looked from my mother to her husband, the smile faded as steadily as the deflating of a balloon. She let out a gasp as she realized what I meant. In the background, my father seemed to be trying to swallow a laugh.

I watched, wondering why everyone was acting so strange. Then I felt a sharp pain on my cheek. "Mama, don't." And another.

"Don't listen to her. I don't know where she heard such a thing. I'll punish her. I swear." She grabbed me by the shoulders and started shaking me. While my head bobbled and I cried, Cy, awake now, stood with his hand over his mouth smirking at my punishment.

"No. Don't." Aunt Shirley grabbed my mother's hands to loose them from me. "She's just a baby." Her cheeks were glistening. Was it because I was looking through wet eyes? No. She was crying, too. "Don't," Aunt Shirley said again, huskily.

My mother couldn't be put off. "I'll kill her. Whoever heard of such a thing!"

Her "rat" stuck out from under her hair. Her face was twisted and ugly. She was so different from her sister. How I wished I were Aunt Shirley's child instead.

Moe stepped forward. "Leave the child alone!"

As suddenly as a radio stops when you pull out the plug, that's how quickly my mother stopped shouting and hitting me.

"It was a mistake," Uncle Moe was saying with a note of finality in his voice. "Let's go, Shirley." To my father he said, "I'll see you on Monday."

They left. As soon as the door was closed in back of them, my mother, who I thought was punishing me only to prove something to Aunt Shirley and Uncle Moe, started again, crying herself as she hit me again and again.

My father was no Uncle Moe. He didn't even try to stop her. Like my mother, I, too, could learn to hate him for being so passive.

That night I fell asleep in my red pinafore. My only comfort was the tea set on my bed. During the night I must have turned on a plate, for in the morning my arm was scratched and, what was worse for me, one of the curly-edged plates was broken.

I shivered, partly from the memory of the little girl who had no idea why she was being beaten and partly from the coldness of the room. My mother was right. They kept these places as cold as death.

There was silence after Moe spoke. We

were waiting for my mother to agree with him that her sister was a saint. I watched my mother's face softening. She must have been figuring it out, what would it hurt to be nice this once?

She smiled and nodded, the change in her expression too abrupt to be anything other than an act. "Oh, yes, a heart of gold."

Some neighbors of my mother's came into the room. With greetings, introductions, kisses, sighs, and shakes of the head, they settled into the couches, experienced at this sort of thing. While my mother spoke to them, Moe turned to Steve and me and spoke to us in a low murmur.

"A heart of gold," he began. "Did you ever hear how I came to marry her?"

I shook my head no, for by now I knew that she really hadn't roped him.

"She was married to a distant cousin of mine, a teacher in the city. From the minute I laid eyes on her, I wanted to get her to marry me. She was some beauty. And her husband was a schlemiel, a mama's boy. A nothing."

"What made her decide to marry you?" I asked. I was curious because I had heard my mother's explanation often enough. *She* figured every few years she should get a promotion. First she was married to a clerk, then a teacher, then a rich business-man.

"Well," Moe was saying, "Cy came down with mastoids when he was a little guy about four years old. Today antibiotics cure it. But then you needed an operation. It was serious. From the beginning, the professor, as I called him, objected. He was a high-school teacher and teachers did well com-pared to everyone else, but he milked a nickel until it hollered and he wasn't going to part with any of his precious money for his wife's kids.

"I knew Shirley, but I couldn't get anywhere with her." He paused, waiting for us to show that we caught on to what he was saying. It seemed obscene for an old man to be talking about *getting somewhere* with a woman so recently dead, but I nodded to encourage him to go on with his tale.

"To make a long story short," he con-tinued, "I told her not to worry. I would pay the bills. I liked her kids. They had spunk. I paid willingly, and after Cy was all better, she moved out on the professor." His eyes misted over. "It was the best thing that ever happened to me."

He's a fool for her was the way I had always heard it from my mother. My poor father, I thought. How could he ever measure to a brother-in-law like Moe?

Cy and his wife came into the room looking serious but not especially grieving. He kissed me on the side of the face, coolly, and I wondered what his accountant's brain was calculating.

We sat talking a few minutes longer. "Let's go," I whispered to Steve when I had the chance. We checked on my mother's ride home and we said our good-byes. It was warm and muggy outside, drizzling slightly, the opposite of the cool, dry air of the chapel.

Walking to the lot, I thought about what Moe had been saying. He had been a wonderful stepfather. In a way, he was Cy's father, for hadn't he saved his son's life? I hoped Cy and Jack would continue to be close to Moe.

I glanced at Steve. He would be a wonderful stepfather, too. He was patient with Barry, and they could talk sports and cars for hours. During the basketball season, Steve often took him to games. Even now, he wasn't disgusted with Barry as I was.

Oh, but where *was* Barry? I glanced at my watch. It was almost ten.

"What's the matter?" Steve asked me.

"I'm worried about Barry. Could we stop off at a phone booth and I'll see if Barry's home. If not, I'd like to go to Suzanne's and see if he's there."

"Jewish mother?" Steve teased as we got into the car.

"I can't help it. He's only seventeen."

Steve smiled at me reassuringly. "It's all right. I understand. Is there anyplace else where he could be?"

I shook my head. "All his other friends live with their parents."

He backed out of the lot.

"All of his friends that I know," I added.

We stopped at a phone booth a few blocks away and I tried the house. No one answered.

I gave Steve Suzanne's address and he turned the car around. As we drove through the streets of Brooklyn, we kept passing groups of teenagers congregated like bugs around a light on every second or third corner. "Wait," I called out, my heart pounding suddenly. "Stop the car. I think I saw him."

Steve pulled up to the curb and I ran out of the car, stumbling in excitement. Let it be him, I thought to myself, and we'll talk about this coincidence for the rest of our lives. Like God sent me to him.

I ran up behind the boy, but as I approached him he turned toward me, finding me staring at him. He wore a similar jacket to Barry's and jeans like all the kids. Otherwise, he didn't look a thing like my son.

"Excuse me," I murmured, feeling foolish. "I thought you were someone else."

I returned to the car.

"If it were Barry, what were you going to say to him?" Steve asked me as he started up the car.

"I don't know. I didn't think about it. I guess I really want to make sure he's all right. He did run off with a certified nut."

"You mean Suzanne?"

"Who else?"

"Yeah. She is a mixed-up kid."

"She's twenty-two," I reminded him. "That's no kid." In fact, even when she *was* a kid, she wasn't.

A picture came into my mind of Suzanne at Nat's funeral. She was a tall, buxom girl of thirteen, looking more like seventeen, with a thin, pointed face like her father's.

Barry had seen his half sister only a few times before. He was fascinated with her, especially with the way she carried on, moaning and sobbing with grief. She sat across the aisle from us and when I put out my hand to touch her arm in comfort before the ceremonies (there were so many people watching), she recoiled from my touch. She leaned against one of her aunts, Nat's oldest sister, and together they looked at me as though I had personally planted the telephone pole that took her father's life. Perhaps they thought I caused his business to fail, too.

I had to put up with it. At least until after the funeral. A few more hours and I would be through with the whole lousy bunch of them. They had never really accepted me.

I wondered about Nat's sisters. I had been ready to leave Nat. Did they know? If the accident had occurred a few months later, I might not even have been sitting here. I wondered if that would have affected his insurance policy.

A feeling of warmth toward Nat filled me. The poor schlemiel. I felt more for him dead at the services than I had for years when he was alive. He had done what he could for me and Barry. In the end, he lived up to his bargain.

"What should I do?" Nat had cried to me only three evenings before. His business failing fast, he was begging me for the money I had saved in my name since our marriage. He wanted me to give it to him to throw after his friends' and sisters' money into a sinking business.

"What should I do?" he cried when I refused. "Kill myself?"

"I have a son to protect. Our son," I told him.

How like a weasel he looked, his cheeks sprouting black little hairs, his beady eyes shining with fear. How could I ever have married him? And to think, not only could he no longer give me what I married him for, but he wanted *my* money.

"What do you want me to do? Should I kill myself?" he repeated.

How could my life have turned out so

poorly? I married him for power, for security, for wealth, and now he had nothing. He *was* nothing. "Don't whine," I said. "At least be a man and stop whining."

He went to his sister's house that night. Driving home, possibly drunk, although I doubted it—I think he would have been cold sober no matter how much he drank beforehand—he crashed into a pole and died instantly.

His sisters didn't speak to me when I saw them at the chapel the night before the funeral. It was to my advantage. They had lent him money without notes. Now let them try to collect.

The day of the funeral I had Barry to fuss over and comfort in public. Later on the cemetery grounds Suzanne, on the path in front of me and Barry, suddenly spun around to face us.

She pointed a finger at Barry. "You're my brother," she stated matter-of-factly.

He was too surprised to reply and she turned around again. She carried on while the rabbi spoke, drowning out his prayers so that not even my son and I, truly the chief mourners, could hear him.

When it was over, I had only one

thought—to get away. From Nat's sisters and his friends and his horrible hysterical daughter. To start anew. With the money from Nat's policy and the sale of our house, I could finally be independent, free. I knew Steve wanted us to get married, dear Steve, but that's not what I wanted. I wanted him, of course, as always, but marriage would have to wait. First, I had to taste freedom. I wanted to build my career, find a new home, help my son adjust to his father's death.

Going home in the air-conditioned limousine, Barry put his head on my shoulder. From his sighs and shakes of his head, I guessed he was thinking of the past. I wasn't. I was picturing the future that lay ahead like a newly-paved road without signs, without markers.

Barry! The name echoed in my consciousness. "What?"

Steve had to repeat himself. "Did Barry ever stay with Suzanne before?"

"He was there a couple of weeks ago, but he never slept there before. *If* he's there now," I added.

We were driving through one of the

fancier sections of Brooklyn. The apartment houses stood like boxes lined up against one another, their lobbies bright, doormen standing in many of them.

We came to another section. It was an Italian section with neat private homes, lawns the size of stamps, trees with little wire fences around them. Squarely in the middle of many of the living-room windows was a lamp or a vase of artificial flowers, but occasionally a religious statue was framed by the open drapes.

Apartment houses became more frequent again. We were on Suzanne's block, straining to see the numbers of the houses. There was one house with garbage pails overflowing at the curb. Some young people were sitting on the steps in front and stood around the entrance. Yes. It was Suzanne's place.

We had to walk through the poeple sitting on the steps.

"And she said—"

"So I told him—"

"Excuse us," I murmured.

Suzanne's name was listed on the mailbox. Third floor.

We walked up. The hall smelled of

unidentified food. The walls were painted a dusky rose. The tiles on the floor might have been pretty once, but now you couldn't see their pattern for the dirt. We came to her door and rang the bell.

"Relax," Steve murmured.

He was right. I was tense. I took a deep breath and moved my neck and shoulders to loosen up. *Please, let him be here,* I prayed silently.

"Who is it?"

That was her voice. At least she was home.

"It's Phyllis Albert and Steve," I called through the closed door.

"Oh. Wait a minute."

There was some talking back and forth going on inside. One latch on the door was opened. Suzanne opened the door and spoke to me over the chain.

"What do you want?"

"Is Barry here?"

"Why?"

She was wearing a bathrobe and slippers. The robe gaped open showing little raised brown spots near her breasts.

Steve glanced at me. I knew he was able to gauge my rising anger.

"Phyllis was worried about him. She'd like to know if he's here."

Suzanne looked behind her. "Are you here, Barry?" she called into the apartment.

Barry shuffled to the door. He was wearing a T-shirt and jeans. He looked sullen.

Tears filled my eyes at the sight of him, but I had another excuse. "My Aunt Shirley died, Barry. The funeral's tomorrow."

"Oh."

I told him the time and place of the funeral, more to fill the silence than in any expectation that he would come.

When I finished, he asked, "Want to come in?"

"All right," Steve answered for us.

Barry unchained the door and moved aside to let us in. The apartment smelled from cheese and cigarette smoke. The furniture was old, stuffed, probably Ruth's. No, she could have afforded better. More probably it was the last tenant's.

"Come on in," Barry said leading us into the little kitchen. "You can meet our friends."

Two men in their twenties were sitting at

the table with Suzanne drinking wine. They could both have been her boyfriends, but I was sure one wasn't.

"This is Mal, Suzanne's boyfriend," Barry said. The young man, square-faced and angry looking, glanced at us. "And this is Richie."

My boyfriend, I mentally ended the sentence for my son.

Richie was a good-looking young man with a neat ash-blond beard and light hair. Unlike Mal, he smiled at us and raised himself in his seat in a gesture of politeness.

"Hello, Mrs. Albert."

His voice surprised me. It was huskier than I had expected. What did I expect? A sashaying fairy? What does it matter how masculine he looks? In bed he does the same damned thing as the most obvious queer.

I forced an answer. "Hello."

He was older than Barry. Years older. That was obvious.

They were sitting around an old metal table. I hadn't seen one like it for years. The kitchen was long and narrow, with one brown-streaked window at the far end that looked as if it had never been opened.

All the apartment I saw was painted a

baby-blue color with strips and circles of white plaster punctuating the walls. The linoleum underfoot had long been worn out. And this is what Barry preferred over his perfect home in the suburbs?

"When are you coming home, Barry?" I asked.

He shrugged, a childish gesture. He couldn't look at me. "I don't know, Ma. I figured you kicked me out yesterday."

"No. I didn't kick you out."

It was the moment to say it. To swallow my pride and apologize. But I looked around. Suzanne was watching me and her tough-looking boyfriend, and the homo, Barry's friend. I couldn't. The words stuck in my throat.

"I didn't kick you out," I repeated. "You belong home."

He looked at Richie. "I—I can't." He seemed abashed. "I promised." He waved a hand in Richie's general direction. Suddenly, the young man began studying his own nails. Guilty?

I addressed myself to him. "Barry should be home. He's only seventeen, you know. You're over twenty-one, aren't you?"

Richie's cool hazel eyes were directly on

mine. "I'm twenty-three, Mrs. Albert."

"Twenty-three? Isn't there a statutory law?" I asked Steve.

"The juvenile has to be under seventeen."

"Oh." I turned back to Richie. "Six years older than my son. Aren't you using him?"

Barry flushed.

Richie cocked his head at me. "We use each other. Like you and your boyfriend here," he said.

Suzanne giggled. "Forget it, Phyllis. Really. He wants to stay here tonight. He can stay as long as he wants."

I could feel the tears again. It must be my hormones changing, I guessed. It was so hard to control my feelings.

"Look, Barry," Steve was beginning. "Your mother is worried about your safety, your health. You're her responsibility. Try to understand *her*."

Barry made a sour face.

"Come on, Steve. We might as well go."

"I'll go to the door with you," Barry murmured to us. With his bright and shining blue eyes and red cheeks and black hair, he was beautiful. Too beautiful, perhaps.

"Good-bye," I said to the others. I turned

and then turned back, hesitating. Well, why not? My son was in her care, it seemed. "Suzanne, you'll look after your brother?"

She chuckled. "My brother's beautiful," she said. She meant something different from what I had been thinking.

Walking into the living room, I tripped over the linoleum, curling like a wave breaking on a beach, at the edges of the room. The place *was* awful.

"How can you stay here?" I whispered.

Barry's eyes flashed. "My friends are here. And my sister. Remember?" His eyes met Steve's. Immediately, he seemed contrite. "I'm OK. Richie takes care of me. You don't have to worry."

He must have read the expression on my face.

"Ma, we l-like each other a lot. You have to accept it."

We stood in a long few seconds' silence at the door.

"He's a schoolteacher," Barry added in his friend's defense.

My son is such a child.

"Do you have enough food? Enough money?" Steve asked him. Steve, the practical one.

"Oh, yes." He thought for a moment. "I could use my allowance."

I gave him his money. He took it and thanked me.

"Good-bye, Ma."

"School's Monday," I reminded him. He was taking Driver's Ed in school. I had to depend on Driver's Ed to get my son home.

He nodded, looking serious and troubled beyond his years.

"Good-bye, Barry." Steve shook his hand.

Barry closed the door and we left. In the hall the smells of cooking and dampness and something else—Lysol, was it?—overcame me. I grabbed Steve's arm.

"Are you all right?"

"Dizzy." That would have to cover nausea, a cold sweat, weak knees. "I need fresh air."

"You'll feel better in a second," he said leading me outside. "And don't worry," he told me once I was sitting and feeling better in the car. "I think Suzanne will take care of Barry."

That's what I'm afraid of, I thought, but it was better not said. Steve was only being kind. What a turnabout, though. After all these years, I had to depend on Suzanne to look after my son.

Until his thirteenth summer, Barry hardly knew his half sister. Those few times her name was mentioned, I always managed to remind him, subtly, of her nastiness: the times she hurt him, her peculiar behavior at their father's funeral. "She's jealous of you. Daddy left her with her mother and married me, and you know how he adored you. He saw you every day, but he only saw her once a week at the most. She was such an unpleasant, ugly little thing, poor kid."

Once I overheard a new friend of his ask him if he had any brothers or sisters.

"No," Barry replied.

"But what about Suzanne?" I asked him out of curiosity when the other boy had gone.

"Her?" He made a face. "I don't call her a sister."

Good, I thought to myself. Except for a birthday card for Barry once a year, we never heard from Nat's family, and that was fine with me. They could all bust for all I cared. The bitches!

Barry was going to spend the two months

following his twelfth birthday in a sleep-away camp a neighbor of mine had recommended highly. Of course, she got a good commission for her recommendation, but the camp looked nice enough from the pictures, the director sounded competent, and it would give Steve and me. the opportunity to have a real vacation—a month in Europe.

It was a complete accident that Suzanne was a counselor in the girls' part of the camp. Later in the year, Suzanne told me how she had reintroduced herself to her half brother. She told the story as though it were a big joke, and the joke wasn't on her.

One day when she was in the mail room, she had spotted a package with the name Albert on it. It was a soccer ball Steve and I sent to Barry from Italy. She realized immediately that the Barry Albert it was addressed to was her brother. But when Barry was asked by another counselor if Sue were his sister, he answered no, never associating *Sue* with his half sister, Suzanne.

He didn't really like camp. It was a cold and wet summer and the smell of rot was everywhere. There was little hot water for the bunks and only the first couple of people to the sinks and showers in the morning got any. Barry made it once. The food was of poor quality. Hash was the most frequent dish served. But the worst thing of all was that the kids didn't seem to like him and the counselors, bored and underpaid, encouraged the contempt.

They made fun of Barry for being good-looking. They called him Prince Charming and mussed his folded clothes and hid his brushes or used them for the dirty floors. He was naturally neat and clean. Up there, those virtues were considered faults.

But if they didn't make fun of him for being handsome and clean, it would have been for being ugly and slobbish or slow or smart. Barry was lucky, in fact. There was one fat kid the counselors called Barrel O' Shit, even, Barry told me, years later, letting the name slip out on Visitors' Day.

One night toward the middle of July, Barry was awakened from a deep sleep by his counselor Al, a gawky, big-nosed college sophomore.

"Listen," he whispered shaking Barry awake, "you got to hide your sister or we'll be fired."

"What?" Barry asked sleepily.

The next thing he knew, someone was lifting up his blankets and diving under them into his bed.

"Shut up," Al warned him.

From downstairs, he heard a voice call, "Al?"

"I'm coming," Al answered. "I'm checking up on one of the kids."

Al moved away from the bed. Barry was trying not to touch the warm body hiding next to him.

Footsteps sounded in the room.

"I could have sworn I saw someone running into this bunk." That was the director of the camp. A circle of light ran up and down the beds. "You didn't see anyone?"

"No. One of the kids called out in his sleep. That's all."

"OK. Get to bed."

The footsteps squeaked on the steps and faded. A door closed.

Sister? Did Al say *sister?* Barry was trying to remember.

Suzanne picked up the covers and sat up. "That was close. This place is a prison," she muttered.

Yes. It was her: older, skinnier. Seen, but

not recognized, in the canteen and mess hall. It was her.

"What are you doing here?" Barry asked. He meant in the camp.

She thought he meant in the bunk. "Come on," she answered him. "Can't you figure out what you got in the boys' camp that I want? Are you a baby?"

Footsteps sounded on the steps again. She threw the covers over her head. The footsteps stopped at Barry's bed.

"Come on out, Sue," Al whispered. "He's gone. We can go back down."

She tossed the covers off her and started to follow Al. After a few steps, she turned back to Barry. "Come see me when you have free time. I'll be in the canteen."

He didn't answer her. He was too confused. He wasn't supposed to like Suzanne. He didn't like Suzanne. Didn't he always make fun of her whenever her name was mentioned. But he did like the girl who jumped into his bed. She was cute and perky and he liked the idea that she singled him out to rescue her. He wanted to think about what she had said to him and what happened from the moment Al woke him, but when he leaned back on his pillow to think, he fell asleep.

When he awoke the next day, his first thought was that it was a dream. He wasn't positively sure it happened until he went to the canteen during his free time and saw Suzanne there.

"That's Barry, my half brother," she said to some waiters she was talking to. (It was Barry's best moment of the summer.) "Isn't he cute?"

"There goes his cherry," one of the waiters joked.

Suzanne laughed, but Barry sensed that it wasn't a nice thing to say. His emotions rose. He would have gladly given up all his carefully acquired baseball cards to protect his sister from whoever made fun of her or hurt her feelings. He sensed her need. He would have plenty of time to comfort her and cry in frustration himself when she couldn't hear him anymore or take comfort from him, but he didn't know it then.

I didn't even know she was in his camp until one cool and cloudy August day when Steve and I drove up there.

Regular Visitors' Day had been when we were in Europe. We needed special permission to come up in the middle of August.

I was anxious to see Barry. His letters had changed since the beginning of the season. He was suddenly more independent. He had stopped all his complaining.

The campgrounds were in the midst of a wooded area. All around, the foliage was a lush, dark green and the smell of pine trees hung in the air over the smells of dampness and rotting. A stone house where the camp owner lived with his family stood guard before the sloping grounds.

I introduced myself as Mrs. Albert to the man who answered my knock. "I'm Barry Albert's mother. And this is my friend, Mr. Scher," I introduced Steve.

"Oh, yes. Mrs. Albert." He seemed embarrassed by Steve. Because we're not married? I wondered. Well, he did live up here most of the year. He could be that provincial. "I guess you'd like to see your children?"

"Child," I corrected him. "One child."

He seemed surprised. "Barry, and what about Sue?"

"Sue? You mean Suzanne Albert?"

"Yes."

I couldn't believe it. The one person I

always tried to keep away from my son. "She has dark hair, dark complexion, about seventeen?"

"Yes. She's here in a special counselor-training program."

"She's my late husband's daughter. What a coincidence."

"You didn't know she was here?"

I shook my head and turned to Steve. "Isn't this the strangest thing?"

The owner left us to page Barry. I asked his wife about my stepdaughter.

"I haven't seen her for years," I explained. "How is she?"

The woman looked from Steve to me without speaking. She obviously couldn't decide how much she should reveal.

"She seemed to be a troubled child the last time we saw her," Steve commented.

The woman raised a hand and let it fall in a gesture of helplessness. "I can't begin to tell you." We must have looked sympathetic because she continued confidentially, "I tell my husband that she's more trouble than she's worth, but once he let her come here, he figures he's got to keep her. We made a special arrangement for her. She's not a regular counselor."

Her husband came back.

"I think Barry's a good influence on Sue, don't you?" she asked him.

Oh, no, I thought. It's good for them, but what did I get myself and Barry into?

There was a knock at the door.

"Come in."

Barry walked in, taller and more mature looking than he had been. He accepted my kiss manfully and put out his hand to shake Steve's.

"Why don't you show your mother and—uh—" he looked away, "her friend your bunk?"

"I want to adjust something on the car. You two go," Steve said to Barry and me. "I'll meet you later."

I went out with Barry and we walked down the tree-lined dirt path to his bunk.

"That's the baseball field," Barry said as we passed near home plate, "and that's where we go for cookouts," he said when we passed some benches and barbecue pits.

I asked him if he had enough warm clothes and what they served for breakfast. He told me about fishing and overnight hikes and the science project. But we were

both thinking about the same thing—
Suzanne.

The path we were on ended in a large circle, an American flag waving on a pole planted in its center. Smaller paths radiated from the center to the bunkhouses and to one larger wooden building.

Barry took a deep breath. Even so, he seemed breathless. "That's my bunk there." His voice was changed. It was excited now. "I want you to meet somebody in the canteen first." He led me across the circle to the walk to the canteen. "Come on," he urged me at the door.

Inside the building it was dark. The smells of wet wood and candy permeated the air. At the far end, barely visible, a young man was playing a tinny-sounding piano. Some other teenage boys were sparring in fun while a couple of girls watched them. A few smaller boys were choosing candy at a stand.

Barry led me to a figure sitting by herself and smoking furiously. "Look, Ma. Suzanne!"

Thank God the owner had prepared me for her, for if I came upon this apparition, Barry's half sister, with only my son's *Look*,

Ma for warning, I might have screamed or cried or even fallen down laughing hysterically. What she looked like!

I had just come back from Europe. I had seen plenty of young girls looking unkempt and uncaring, but how different Suzanne was. She was much too thin. Her eyes were expressionless. And her dark hair was matted and dusty.

"Suzanne!" I exclaimed.

She chose to ignore me. "You brought her here?" she asked Barry.

Barry smiled weakly, embarrassed, and looked from her to me. Out of sympathy for him, I'd have to try to save the situation. If I could.

"Hello, Suzanne," I began, pretending that she was normal. "Isn't it something that you're here, too. What a coincidence!"

She waved her hand in front of her face as though my words were written on the air and she was erasing them. "Why'd you bring her here?" she asked Barry. The ash from her cigarette fell to the floor.

Barry didn't bother to answer her. Instead, he turned to me. "Come on, Ma, I'll show you my bunk." To her, he murmured, "We're going."

138

I marveled at the ease with which he spoke to her. They seemed to share a cryptic language of their own, like adults who knew each other for years, or contemporaries—though Suzanne, five years older than Barry, was on the brink of womanhood while my son was still a child—or like brother and sister.

"Good-bye, Sue," I said to her before I left with Barry. She didn't answer. Already she was sitting as she had been when we came in, slumped about herself, smoking automatically, the cigarette her link to the outside world.

We were outdoors where it was cool and green. "What's wrong with her?"

Barry glanced at me, worried. "What do you mean?

"There's obviously something wrong with her. Either she's crazy or on drugs."

He caught his lower lip between his teeth and tossed his hair out of his eyes. A line appeared between his eyebrows.

"What are we gonna do?" he asked.

"Do?" I flinched from the word. Being involved with her was the last thing I wanted for Barry and me. She was bad news. She never was anything except trouble. "What do you mean, Barry?"

We stood in front of his bunk. Kids and counselors went in and out stepping around us.

"You're right," he said, his voice a husky whisper. "She's sick, I think. She needs help. They wanted to make her go home for good a few weeks ago, but her mother pays for her to come here and Sue didn't want to go home. She just laughs at them here, and they can't do anything. But she's not happy."

"Listen, Barry," I put a hand on his arm to stop him from running away from what I had to say, "you can't get involved with her. She'll drag you down. You know she was always jealous of you."

"No." He shook off my hand. "I don't want to hear it. Anyway, it's too late. I am involved with her. She's my sister and she needs me."

We waited for a boy from his bunk to pass out of hearing. "I—I love Sue." With that, he ran into the bunk.

Love? I thought. What does a boy his age know about love?

I followed him into his bunk and he showed me his bed and his cubbyhole, the tooled pictures and woven place mats and lanyards he had made. It felt strange playing mother and child after what he had said, but how could we change?

"Can I have this picture? I'd like to frame it for the playroom."

"Sure."

"Thanks."

When we were out of the bunk again and hurrying back to the main house, I finally got the chance to say what was on my mind from the moment I saw Suzanne. "Promise me one thing, Barry. Don't take drugs. Even if she begs you to."

"Oh, Ma." Like the child he still was, he ran a few feet away from me in consternation. "Why do you say that? Of course I wouldn't. Why would she want me to?"

There were only two and a half weeks left of the camp season. I'd have to leave him for two and a half weeks, seventeen days. I would have liked to ask the director to get rid of her or to keep Barry and her separated, but I couldn't. Barry was acting differently than he ever had before with me. He wouldn't stand for my coming between them.

In seventeen days, with God's help, Barry

would come home to Long Island. Suzanne would pick up her life in the city again, and they would drift apart. I would have to wait out the seventeen days.

As it turned out, they were separated sooner than I thought. Only a few days after my visit, Suzanne decided to leave on her own. She told Barry she was going home, but she didn't make it back there until weeks later. And the one who suffered most when she was gone was Barry.

At first, he called me from camp sounding on the verge of tears. "Where is she? Why don't they find her?" With his next call, he begged me to speak to Ruth. Would I please tell her to call him the minute she hears from Suzanne?

He got a postcard from Suzanne at camp. When he got home from camp, he waited all morning for the mailman and all afternoon until he could call Ruth to check with her. Then just as he was beginning to come around and get busy with his schooling and other activities, Suzanne returned. The season of Barry's half sister was upon us.

Having dropped out of school in the springtime, she had nothing to keep her at home. After a miserable week in her own house, Barry convinced her that she would be happier at ours.

She arrived one summery afternoon by taxi (Ruth really must be desperate to get rid of her, I thought) looking years older and even skinnier than she had in camp. She was distracted and weepy. Barry told her to sleep over. She did. And then another night and another.

"Ma, don't send her away," Barry begged me one morning. "She's so depressed." (*Depressed.* That was *her* word. I never heard him use it before.) "I'm the only one she can talk to. Just another day. Please."

So she stayed on. During the day when Barry was in school she napped—she hardly slept at night—and she moped around. She couldn't seem to concentrate on anything for more than a minute or two—not watching television or looking through magazines or helping me with the cleaning or the wash. In the middle of whatever she was doing, she seemed to forget what she had started. Or she would get disgusted and give up. Sometimes, she would go off, and before I knew it she would be moaning and weeping and I couldn't help her at all. A few times, she began a

143

long, involved story, but I soon found out that her stories had no ending and no point.

I put off my appointments until later in the week. And I warned Barry, *She's got to go*. She was making me dread my own house.

Steve came to the house one evening and tried to speak to her. Then he turned to Barry and Barry, for the first time, answered Steve back.

Steve got angry. "What do you know about mental illness? The end result of depression without treatment is suicide. Would you feel better about that?" he asked him.

I made up my mind. Even Barry had to agree, as much as he hated the idea. I called Ruth and told her to come and get her daughter. "I suggest an institution. I don't think you'll be able to help her at home."

Ruth came within the hour looking old and tired and mean. Her husband, a short man with a half circle of gray around his head, spoke to Suzanne as though she were a naughty little girl.

"Now we've been very patient," he told her as she sat holding herself in her arms and rocking back and forth. She didn't hear him.

"Don't worry," Barry told her. "I won't let anyone hurt you. You have to go for your own good. You'll feel better soon, you'll see, and we'll go for long walks. We'll go swimming and skiing like we talked about, and camping."

Though he made more sense than her stepfather, I don't think she heard him either. Her eyes were blank. Her rocking continued.

Two attendants came for her with an ambulance. She let them lead her away as some children from the neighborhood stood around and watched. When they closed the doors, Barry sobbed and ran into the house.

Poor Barry. To have found his sister so suddenly, and then to lose her so soon. How much he had changed in a few months. Before he went to camp, his greatest concern had been making the Police Boys' Club all-star basketball team. Through Suzanne, he had had a glimpse into hell, and what's more, he would follow her there if he thought it would help her.

She stayed in the hospital for over a year. It was a respite for me. I hoped Barry's feelings for her would diminish the longer she was away, but they didn't. He wrote to her before she was sane enough to read his letters. He planned holiday excursions for her and himself, and the holidays came and went without any word from Suzanne. Then, after a few more months, she was better. He was able to speak to her on the phone and visit her at the hospital and, later, at her home when she came home for weekends. I had warned him that her treatment might diminish her memory of him. After all, she knew him well only for a short time before her breakdown. He was doubly pleased when she remembered him, thrilled with any sign that she was coping.

It took him hours by train and bus to see her, but he never complained. He never seemed irked by her or discouraged after seeing her, either. He reminded me of a bridegroom in the first blush of marriage, and I was the doubting mother-in-law from whom all my son's bride's faults were kept secret.

She was released a few months after Barry's Bar Mitzvah. I still was telling Barry what to eat and how to dress, but I couldn't tell him anything about Suzanne— to this day, I thought, remembering the night before.

"What's the matter?" Steve asked.

"Suzanne. I was thinking about her."

The lights of the highway looked like a rhinestone chain through the droplets on the windshield. "I speak to the woman, but I see the child I hated when I was a young girl."

Steve took his eyes off the road to glance at me quizzically.

"I guess I haven't been fair to her," I confessed. "She cares for Barry and that means a lot."

I sat there for a long while thinking about us all. It was easy to keep the ideas and values of long ago, easier than to change. But times changed and people changed. Even Suzanne. Even me.

"I was a kid when I married Nat," I said. "I didn't know what end was up. Believe me, we both would act differently if we could do it all over again. Me and you, I mean."

For a second, he looked serious. But then his features softened into a smile. "My offer still holds."

I slid closer to him. It was good to feel him

next to me, to know that he was there. And he wanted me even without knowing about the baby.

If only I hadn't made such a mess with Barry. I put my head on Steve's shoulder. Maybe, I thought. If I can get straightened out with Barry—after he comes home. . . .

It would be so easy. But there was the baby, the one I was carrying. Another, perhaps, too, for Steve wanted a family. He deserved one.

I pictured myself sitting with young mothers on a park bench. They might think it was my grandchild. And the baby would get up in the middle of the night and cry and I would have to go to it. Babies spit up and dirty their diapers and need constant attention. In the morning, there would be new lines around my eyes. Steve would go off to work, as always, and I would have to stay home. If I wanted to go out, I'd need a baby-sitter.

Barry. Wouldn't he be embarrassed by his mother's baby? As if he didn't have enough troubles.

"What are you thinking about?" Steve asked.

"Nothing," I answered, putting my hand

over my belly, welcoming the feeling of warmth. Truly, it could be nothing. And it could be everything.

That night, Steve fell asleep before me. He snored and I poked him until he turned over and stopped snoring. He was lying on his side, the hairs on his chest showing through his open pajama top. Yellow and silver they were, like fuzz. When I first met Steve, he had a couple of light hairs on his chest. Now so many were silver. He was getting old. He wanted children of his own. How much longer would he wait?

Sunday

I woke up just as a bubble of nausea in my chest started making its way down to my stomach.

Ugh. My eighth day. Maybe it was my period coming on. I went, heavy legged and feeling sick, to the bathroom. No period.

Just nausea. Ugh.

I retched over and over, running the water loud to cover the sound. I had nothing to throw up. When I stopped the retching, I looked at myself in the mirror. I looked like hell. A thirty-six-year-old woman has no right to get pregnant.

They'd laugh and gossip about me: my neighbors, my customers. Some might be sincere. They'd hope for the best for me and be concerned, but for most of the people who knew me, it would be a juicy tidbit, something to savor with their coffee.

My cousins. What would they say? Cy would be scandalized. He was so conventional. I could joke about it with Jack. He'd understand.

And Barry? He'd be embarrassed. Maybe he'd like the idea of a half brother or sister. Another one. Suzanne? I couldn't guess about her anymore.

I began to retch again.

I was never sick with Barry. I glowed. Nat couldn't get over it. He treated me like a queen, and I played the role for all it was worth. I splashed cold water on my face, and remembered.

*　　　*　　　*

154

I thought a baby would justify our marriage. At last, I would shut up his bitchy sisters. They'd have to be nice to me once there was a child.

I was young, innocent, vulnerable. They didn't have the nerve to say anything about me to Nat, they wouldn't dare, but I knew that they blamed me for the breakup of Nat's first marriage. We came home from our honeymoon to be greeted with a phone call from Nat's older sister.

He answered the phone, starting to chat, and then his expression changed. "Oh my God. What a crazy thing to do!" He held a hand over the phone and whispered to me, "Ruth tried to commit suicide. Thank God they got to her in time."

My honeymoon ended with that call. I sat down hard on our new living-room chairs and tried to figure it out.

She did it for sympathy, of course, and Nat's bitchy sister couldn't wait to tell us. They were always on her side against me even though their brother had spoken to a lawyer about a divorce even before I went to work for him.

Aunt Shirley had an expression, "Don't confuse the issue with logic."

Their sympathy lay with their niece. They never got along well with Ruth, Nat told me, until she became the outraged wife and mother. But, wait. I had a way of winning, too. I would be a perfect wife to Nat. Beautiful, young, intelligent, I would nevertheless live for my husband and, most of all, for my children. I would have beautiful children, lots of them (and my sisters-in-law would marvel, How does she manage so well?). They would be perfect, my children. Boys, of course. Maybe a girl or two.

There was a knock at the door.

"Phyll, are you all right?"

I jumped. It was Steve.

"I'm OK. Go back to bed."

"It's eight," he said through the door. "We better start getting ready."

Of course. The funeral. How was I ever going to get through it?

I took a quick shower, put on makeup and fixed my hair before I went inside to make breakfast. I felt better. Steve was washing up now.

Psychiatrists say there's no such thing as an accidental pregnancy, I mused, as I waited for the water to boil for our coffee. Steve was the one who took care of birth control. The pills had given me headaches, so I quit taking them. Once the rubber was broken when we were finished, but that was last year. I douched with lemon juice and water until my insides puckered, and I didn't get pregnant then. He sometimes penetrated me before he put on a condom, but he never reached a climax inside me with nothing on. Not that I knew of. And I wasn't going through my changes. I was sure of that. I was always as regular as the sunrise.

"Is it your period?" Steve asked over his coffee.

"Maybe. I may be getting it." Now why did I say that? I wondered right after blurting it out. He'll keep on asking me if I got it yet. Then what was I going to tell him?

He looked at me oddly. What was he thinking? I got busy cleaning off the dishes.

A half hour later, for the second time in two days, I wrote a note to Barry telling him that we were going to be in Brooklyn. I still couldn't bring myself to sign it with *Love*.

We were on the highway again. It was going to be a scorcher later on in the day, but this was early, and it was still pleasant. The air seemed cleaner after last night's rain. Even the grass looked greener.

"Where's everyone going?" I asked Steve. It was early Sunday morning, yet a long string of cars stood without moving in the opposite lane. It was easy to forget that there were people in those cars. They seemed more like metal monsters crawling on rubber feet.

My mother was waiting outside her apartment building when we pulled up.

"Do you have a scarf for your hair?" she asked. "I have an extra one."

She was holding a pretty black lace scarf. Always proper. Always prepared.

"Thanks." I didn't want it. "They usually give out those little squares of lace."

"This is so much nicer. How can you compare? Here." She thrust the scarf at me. It was easier to take it than to argue with her. I accepted it dutifully.

Steve smiled at me. He knew how my mother bugged me.

"I simply can't believe it," she said as she settled herself in the backseat. "It was a

Sunday like this when we buried your father. Only cooler then. Remember?"

Of course I remembered, although I was only a child at the time. It was during the war. My father, though, was 4F. "Our luck is changing," was the way my mother put it.

He was doing well driving a cab. (His super's job went to an old retired man, partly feeble and almost senile.) My mother worked at temporary jobs "to help the war effort," she said, but the money was good and she could choose her hours. The day we moved from our apartment in Uncle Moe's building was, she liked to say, the proudest day of her life.

The apartment house she moved to was the same one she still lived in, but it was new and elegant then, and it was ours, without any strings attached. I wasn't the super's daughter anymore.

Dad left for work as usual one Friday morning.

"Bring home jujubes, Daddy."

"I'm playing Mah-Jongg tonight. So be home by nine."

Sometime in the late afternoon, we got a phone call. It lasted less than five minutes. When it was over, my mother was a widow and I found myself fatherless.

He was killed in a holdup in broad daylight, and no one saw anything. They never found his murderer.

I remember a neighbor at the funeral services shaking his head and muttering "Poor son of a bitch" about the man in the closed coffin. I always hated that man afterward. As I grew older and though about the stranger who lived with my mother and me and the waste of his life, I had to agree. Those five words summed it all up. Harry Goldman, my father.

"Oh, I forgot to tell you." My mother's voice broke the chain of memories. "Barry called," she said. "He's coming to the funeral."

"He doesn't have a suit." The words were out of my mouth before I had a chance to think.

Steve shook his head. "When are you going to learn, Phyll?" he remarked in a low voice. "I thought you were worried about him."

"I am. And I'm glad he's coming but . . ."

"Then there are no *but's*. What does it matter what he's wearing?"

Naturally Steve would say that, I

thought. He was the world's worst dresser. If I wanted him to look decent, I had to pick out his clothes for him. Even before his graduation from law school, he always took me shopping with him. I couldn't answer him now.

We were at a red light. It changed, and Steve spoke loud enough for my mother to hear. "It's thoughtful of Barry to come."

There was a few seconds' silence. Then from the back, my mother murmured, "Steve, you're a good man."

His eyes crinkled in a smile.

I glanced back at her. She seemed embarrassed that she had spoken out. It reminded me of another time she had tried to advise me, when Barry was about six.

My mother had started a speech on conventional morality and responsibility to Nat, and I had cut her off angrily.

"Don't tell me what to do. You were so thrilled when I married Nat. And I hate him. I was crazy to marry him. I would divorce him in a minute if I knew I could keep Barry." It sounded logical enough, and it made my mother feel guilty, but it wasn't completely true. I didn't hate Nat. I didn't love him either, but he was tolerable, even convenient. He left me alone to do what I wanted. I could endure him until the inevitable day when I would divorce him. In the meanwhile, I was taking courses in interior design and meeting Steve several times a week in Manhattan.

At home, I lived a life of comfort. Money doesn't buy happiness, but it was fun to discover all the things it could buy. For one thing, I redecorated our home. I liked experimenting with fabrics and furnishings. I learned from my mistakes. Some of them were costly, but Nat didn't mind.

I learned to appreciate good things from French cooking to crystal that caught and reshaped the light. When I was growing up, I used to think it was crazy to buy anything other than the cheapest brand of an item. Now I started to look for strength and design and durability, for the subtle difference that made one stand out among many. Objects from a can opener to a recliner to a set of stainless-steel flatware suddenly fascinated me. My tastes changed. My understanding grew.

I came to love the city. It represented the other part of me—the part that was stretching and growing. I could lose myself in the city and I could find parts of me I never knew existed.

I would have to be aggressive if I wanted to be successful in business, so I tried being aggressive and poised and more confident than I actually felt. It worked. In my classes, the other students asked me for my advice and my teachers encouraged me. "You're a natural," they told me.

So what my mother had told me wasn't entirely wrong. She had only underlined what she herself had missed.

"Look at your Aunt Shirley," she used to say. "While I'm praying for a seat on the subway, she's just lifting her soft little leg out of the tub. Then breakfast, served up by Mattie, and how does milady spend the day? Shopping. *Marketing*, she calls it."

One evening when I had been out of high school a few months and working in Nat's office, he drove me home. I had put in overtime. Overtime with him meant fifteen minutes of work stretched to three hours while he playfully tried to grab or fondle me unawares. My mother and Aunt Shirley happened to be standing at the window and they saw him kiss me good night in the car.

It was only a peck on the lips, but Aunt Shirley was waiting for me when I got upstairs.

"You let a married man kiss you?"

"Oh, Aunt Shirley," I replied. "He's separated from his wife. He's getting a divorce."

"They all say that."

"Don't worry about him," I answered. "I can turn him on and off like a radio."

"Just make sure he doesn't plug you in."

"Aunt Shirley!" I flushed with embarrassment, but I giggled, too. My aunt was so outspoken.

She might have doubted it, but I really did have power over Nat. It was easy when you didn't get emotional over someone. Steel with Nat. Putty for Steve (damn him).

Nat had such old-fashioned ideas. A girl was bad or a girl was good. There was no in-between. I was a good girl. Any little feel I allowed him—and I was smart enough not to allow him many—was greatly appreciated.

Dates with boys my own age had been disastrous. Since I broke up with Steve I had gone out on two dates. The first was with a medical student I met at a local pool who thought he was God's gift to the female sex. He invited me to his parents' home; they were away for the summer, and directly after pretzels and beer, he led me into his bedroom.

"What else is there to do?" he asked me.

There was some fascination in his utter lack of interest in me as a person and he did sound experienced. What did I have to lose? I consented.

We took off each other's clothes. I had never done that with Steve. Then he playfully named the parts of my body poking and "testing" them while I pretended to memorize the Latin names. That was fun, but then he grabbed me, and with the prophylactic still intact on the night table, came all over my thighs. I kept gagging, washing myself off.

He drove me home in silence and I slammed the car door angrily behind me when I left him. What a clod!

My one other date was made for me by a girl in the office, with her brother. He was a tall, geeky boy, as impressed with me as I was unimpressed with him. He took me to a fancy restaurant to eat. (At least I thought it was fancy then, and so did my mother. A couple of years later when I went back there with Nat, although everything was the same, it was quite ordinary.) We went to the movies after dinner, and he kept trying to put his arm around me while I shook him off. I didn't kiss him good night either.

He called many times after that, but I didn't want to go out with him. Word got around the office that I was cool.

A few weeks later, Nat, Mr. Albert, handed me a container of coffee on my break and remarked, "You know it's good to find a nice, respectable girl like you."

I didn't know what he meant.

"You know," he explained, "with high moral standards."

"Oh, yes," I replied, finally understanding, my face a mask while I choked back a laugh.

"Stay as sweet as you are."

I smiled a Mona Lisa smile. That was my new role—sweet Miss Innocence.

At night, trying to fall asleep, I'd try to count the number of times Steve and I had had intercourse. Twice a day when we had the house to ourselves, and when I was menstruating, he came between my breasts. What did it matter? I loved him. I still would take him back if he wanted me, and if he asked my forgiveness—and I would waive the last part.

One evening in the fall when I was working overtime and Nat, half joking, kept trying to feel my behind whenever I got up, he suddenly asked, "You're a virgin, aren't you?"

My face turned red. What a nerve he had! I was beginning to believe in my innocence myself.

"Mr. Albert," I replied. "Don't ask me to work late with you if you're going to get fresh with me." Tears came to my eyes.

The little man saw them and hopped about in distress. "I'm sorry. I forget how young you are. I don't mean to insult you. Listen. Forget it. Forget what I said. All right? Please."

The whole scene was ludicrous. I looked away. He was a gentleman for the rest of the evening.

The next day, he apologized again, and he added something I was going to hear for the next couple of months. "I'm going to have a surprise for you at Christmas."

A surprise. I had had enough surprises from Steve and the medical student.

Nat did give me a voluntary raise that week. Ten dollars. I was making as much as a girl there two years longer than me, and more than I deserved. But not enough to let him grab me.

Still, something told me to play it cool. He brought Suzanne to the office a few weeks later. She was dressed in a fancy green coat and matching dress. The color was terrible on her with her dark skin and mousy brown hair, but I cooed and fussed over her as if she were Shirley Temple. I made a chain of paper clips for her and let her touch the keys of my typewriter. She was fascinated with the letters that appeared on the paper. I took her to the ladies' room, and when I went on my break in the afternoon, I brought her back a malted and refused reimbursement. When she left, I kissed her good-bye.

On his return, Nat was beaming. "I'm glad my two best girls get along so beautifully," he told me.

I still didn't know what he was planning. He had taken me out to dinner several times to restaurants with cloths on the tables, carpeting on the floor, and wine lists to order from. I was embarrassed by my ignorance. He thought it was cute.

Afterward, in the car, he usually tried to get a hand up my dress or on my breast. He reminded me of the boys I knew before Steve. When I had known him awhile, I let him pet me, my eyes closed, thinking of Steve, but I never let him go any further than petting.

It was so easy to stop him. Even after he had just tickled me to an orgasm (you took what you could get, I figured), I was still able to jump away from him and insist, "No. No more, please. I'm saving myself for my husband."

Guiltily he'd agree while I marveled that I had found the one man in all of New York who would believe such bullshit.

"Now don't forget, I'm planning a special surprise for you for Christmas," he reminded me one evening in early December before he dropped me off at my house.

"You won't tell me what it is?"

"Nope. It's a secret."

It was possible it was a funny gift—a stuffed animal or something silly like that. He did think of me as a child.

Perhaps he was planning something expensive, a fur jacket he'd expect me to earn. Well, screw him! I smiled to myself when I realized the pun. No, I wouldn't screw him for a fur jacket. I'm no whore. But on the other hand, what did I ever get from Steve and that crumb in Manhattan Beach, the medical student, except aggravation? And a thrill. It was easy to forget that part of it when it was over.

Would I be Nat's mistress? He'd have to be most persuasive! Most generous. I was, after all, half his age.

I helped to decorate the dark, somber office for the Christmas party: streamers and balloons, delicatessen sandwiches and whiskey in paper cups. The record player blared out "From Here to Eternity" and a mambo, "Eh, Mambo."

Bob, an outside salesman, grabbed me to dance with him, but Nat's deliberate, dirty look stopped him. He dropped me in the middle of a step.

"Since when does he own me?" I indignantly demanded of Josephine, my best friend in the office. We were in the ladies' room where it was cold and ugly, and I angrily squeezed out the wet sponge for the pancake makeup I used. "What a nerve!"

Here it was Christmas. Nat was good at

giving out dirty looks to a guy who just wanted to dance with me, but where was the present he promised me? The creep.

"He has no claim on me," I told Josephine after I blotted my lipstick on a piece of toilet paper. "Just because I went out with him a couple of times? I can dance with whoever I want."

Josephine clucked in sympathy, but she was probably wishing she had my problems. When we went back to the party, Nat came over to try to jolly me out of a bad mood. I wanted him to know that I was annoyed. What was he to me?

"I'll take you home tonight, OK?" he asked later when no one was in listening distance.

I hesitated, wishing I had arranged transportation with someone else. I wanted to be independent, but not if it meant taking the train and a bus in the cold.

"Please."

"Oh, all right," I agreed pouting.

Everyone got his bonus, including me, for exactly the sum Josephine told me to expect, and they all left. I put on my coat and waited for Nat. He was turning off all the lights except for the one at my desk.

Fumbling in his inside pocket, he finally took out a tiny box.

He handed it to me. "Here."

It was jewelry, of course. Earrings or a pin, I guessed. It never occurred to me . . .

It was a diamond solitaire, square—over three carats, I could tell.

My mother would be so proud. It was the nicest ring I ever saw, bigger than the one my cousin Jackie gave his girl—that one cost two thousand—nicer than any of my friends'. As nice, yes, as nice as Aunt Shirley's.

I slipped it on my finger. Just a little too big. "It's beautiful," I exclaimed.

When I glanced up from admiring it, Nat planted his round, soft lips on mine. I kissed him with my mouth closed.

"My divorce is coming through soon. Will you wait for a few months and then we can get married? Will you marry me?"

It seemed impossible that all this was happening to me. Here I was in the office I worked in every day. The oil company's calendar on the wall behind me, the light fixture with one bulb out above me, my own desk only a foot away. Here was the president of the company, a man with eleven or twelve employees, including me, a man I hadn't given a thought to when I came here a few months ago except to notice that he was short and middle-aged and seemed nice enough for a boss. And now he was proposing marriage to me, giving me a ring worth thousands.

How the ring sparkled with a million lights. If I married Nat, I would be rich—me, the super's daughter.

"It's just as easy to marry a rich boy as a poor boy." That was one of my mother's favorite sayings. There was only one thing wrong—he was no boy. No, two things. I didn't love him.

"I don't know," I told Nat. "Let me think about it."

He put his arm around me again.

Aunt Shirley would jump and laugh with excitement. The things she could teach me—about silver and china and diamonds. Nat pressed closer. And Steve, I thought. It would serve him right to find out.

Nat smelled of liquor from the party. He kissed me again. My right hand was on Josephine's desk. It moved and I mussed up some of her papers.

Think of the ring, I told myself. The smell

of the liquor, the closeness in the room, and the dim light began to affect me. I couldn't gag. Think of the ring.

"What are you doing?" Steve asked, glancing at my hands.

I was twisting my engagement ring. It still sparkled on my finger though I had come close to selling it.

"Nothing," I answered him. "I was just thinking."

"About what?"

"About Nat and how we became engaged. I guess it's the funeral that makes me think of him."

My mother sighed from the back of the car. "So many funerals I've gone to. I wonder if mine will be next."

I turned around in alarm. "Are you feeling all right?"

She shrugged. "I guess."

"Now you're telling me the truth?" Out of the corner of my eye, I could see Steve smiling at the shrillness in my voice. He often said that my mother and I had reversed our roles.

"Don't worry about me," she said. "I was just talking." She paused. "You know," she said speaking with sudden animation, "I remember one funeral we went to, I was sitting next to Shirley in the chapel and I told her I hope I never have to go to another funeral. She laughed out loud. 'There's only one way to avoid them,' she said. 'Personally, I'd rather go to someone else's.'"

I chuckled.

"That sounds like her," Steve commented.

"It does," I agreed. That started another thread of thought. "Do you remember how we once met Aunt Shirley downtown?"

He seemed to be thinking.

"Many years ago," I reminded him. "You were working for that firm in midtown. I was going to school for design."

He smiled. "It was a hundred years ago?"

"Now you've got it." I turned to my mother in the back. "Did Aunt Shirley ever mention to you that she met me and Steve in New York once?" I had been curious about that before. "Nat was still alive. Barry was about seven then?"

"She met you before I did, Steve?" my mother asked.

Steve nodded. "Yes."

I had been going with him for years then,

ever since we had met in the country. I typed his final law note for him and waited with him for the newspaper listing the students who had passed the bar exam. I treated him to lunches when he was earning forty dollars a week as a law clerk and when he opened his first office, I bought him a typewriter as a gift.

There was a time I was going to divorce Nat. To make sure that I could keep Barry, Steve advised me to hire detectives to discover Nat in an act of adultery. Since I hadn't had anything physical to do with him for ages, I assumed he must have someone somewhere. Even a prostitute would be good enough. I was wrong.

A mild heart spasm he suffered must have scared him enough to give up sex for good. If we had discussed it, he probably would have told me. Unfortunately, we never discussed it, and it took close to a thousand dollars to find out.

When that didn't work, Steve suggested that I make life miserable for Nat. I couldn't. He was such a good-hearted schmo. He took such crap from me and asked so little in return, I couldn't be deliberately nasty. Besides, Steve wasn't earning enough to support the both of us, anyway.

I was open in my dates with Steve. Someday, I was sure, I would meet a friend or a relative of Nat's face-to-face and word would get back to him. It never happened.

But one day while I was window-shopping with Steve in Manhattan after lunch, there was my Aunt Shirley walking briskly in our direction. She didn't notice me. I could have turned away. Steve was intent on looking in the window and didn't even look as though he were with me. I had a decision to make.

Of all the people I knew, the one person I would have liked most to meet Steve was my Aunt Shirley. I glanced at him. He was handsome, intelligent looking even though his suit was cheap and his shoes were scuffed. (How many times I had told him how that annoyed me!) What the hell. I loved him. How could you compare Nat to him? When people who met us assumed that Steve was my husband (I wore a wedding band), I rarely corrected them. I felt good when they thought we were married. I was proud of Steve. And now Aunt Shirley would know who I really belonged with.

"Aunt Shirley!"

She jumped, startled, and we laughed. We kissed hello, her arm flung around me in her usual enthusiastic way. Steve was watching us from the next window, unsure of how I wanted him to act.

"What are you doing? Are you here by yourself?" she asked.

"No," I said loud enough for Steve to hear. "I want you to meet a friend of mine."

I led her to Steve who pivoted around to us slowly. She reddened slightly; her head jerked almost imperceptibly. Then she smiled graciously, her capped teeth white against her carefully brushed on lipstick. "Hello."

I wanted her to know he wasn't the date of an afternoon, that he was my lover for a long, long time. I didn't know quite how to say it. "I know Steve from my high-school days."

"Really?" She studied him. There seemed to be no embarrassment between them. I knew there wouldn't be.

"I see," she added.

She did. There was little else for me to say about him. I asked her about Jack's new baby, her first grandson, and she asked about Barry. Then she kissed me again and shook Steve's hand.

"Take good care of my niece," she told him.

"I will." He smiled at me affectionately. "Don't worry."

We watched her walk off until she was hidden by other pedestrians.

"Why did you do that?" Steve asked me out of curiosity.

"I wanted her to know. I wanted someone from my family to meet you. I *am* proud of you, you know."

"I think you confused her."

We were walking again. Always rushing, it seemed. Steve was going back to the office. I had an afternoon class. We never had enough time together.

"I don't know if she realized exactly where I fit in," Steve was saying.

"Aunt Shirley?" I scoffed. "She knows. Believe me, she knows."

"She never told me," my mother remarked from the back of the car. "She never told me she met you with Phyllis, Steve, not even after . . ." She stopped. She had almost mentioned Nat. She bore my guilt for me, my mother did.

The trail of her thoughts was a clear path that led to what she said next. "And now it's Shirley's funeral. I can't believe it."

She began to cry quietly, with soft, muted little sounds as we drove up to the funeral home. Steve stopped the car. I got out quickly to help my mother out of the back. She was heavy. It was hard for her to move.

"I'll park and meet you inside," Steve murmured to me.

I nodded.

The street air was oppressively hot and heavy. My mother leaned against me before she straightened up, her skin clammy against mine. A wave of nausea hit me. No, I told myself swallowing hard to keep from being sick.

Next to me, my mother was walking with difficulty. So spry and talkative all along, but faced with the reality of her sister's death, she had suddenly aged.

I opened the door to the chapel. The air inside was cold, dry, odorless, a relief from the outside. There were strangers standing around. For a second, I was confused, until I realized that there must be other funeral services going on. As if my mind had been read, a slight man in a dark suit stepped toward us.

"Which funeral service?"

I told him and he directed us to the correct room. He was as fitted for the part as a Hollywood actor. I found myself smiling at the thought. How Aunt Shirley would have laughed at him. He wouldn't have liked her with her clear, loud laugh, her made-up doll's face. In looks, in clothing, in demeanor, they were opposites.

We went to the room he pointed out. Moe and the immediate family, some neighbors I knew, and some unfamiliar people were there.

I kissed Moe, and Jack sitting next to him. I didn't have to say anything. They knew I loved her. For a long moment, Jack held my hand, shaking his head with emotion. He had been crying.

Poor Jack. A large, handsome man, he had really given Shirley a hard time a few years back—and his ex-wife, and their children. An inveterate gambler, he went through all his money and then borrowed thousands more from Moe to pay his gambling debts.

He swore he'd learned his lesson, kept away from racetracks and card games, and he insisted that Moe take out money from his paycheck every week (he worked for his stepfather) for repayment of his debt. Shirley paid for his visits to a psychiatrist, and when his marriage started to flounder, she paid for her daughter-in-law's treatment, too. For a while, things seemed better between Jack and his wife. Then, unexpectedly, there was some trouble in some of Moe's apartment houses. Jack couldn't collect the rents.

"They're having some sort of strike," he told his stepfather. He insisted that Moe let him handle the problem himself. Of course, within a few days, Moe checked with some tenants and discovered that the missing rents had been paid to Jack. When he tried to contact his stepson, Jack was gone. He stayed away for over two years.

Shirley was distraught. "I don't give a damn what he did," I remember her telling my mother. "Money can always be replaced."

Moe didn't try to pursue him though Jack had embezzled tens of thousands of dollars over many months. When he finally returned, he was humbled and broke, without a family—his wife divorced him—without friends—he owed them all money—without a job. A few thousand dollars from his mother settled his most urgent debts. He got a job without much responsibility and learned to live a much quieter, much duller life than before.

His mother never threw it up to him. Once when she came with my mother to visit me, and Barry returned home after school, she hugged him saying, "Isn't it wonderful when they come home. When they're away, you're incomplete."

We knew what she meant.

Cy and his wife were sitting next to Jack. I bent over them and kissed them both lightly. "She was so full of life," I murmured.

They nodded in agreement, but I was sorry I had said anything. I hated to make small talk especially when I felt something so deeply. Well, Cy always made me feel awkward. I think he disapproved of me. He was an accountant—frugal, money conscious, sober, and hardworking. He always seemed to be counting to himself. But when his brother was in trouble, I recalled, he helped Jack.

"And you know how Cy loves money," was the way Shirley put it. "But that's a twin brother. They always fought, but they would share their lifeblood with one another."

Cy had been playing his role as protector, worrier, cautious one for as long as I could remember. Now he looked up toward the doorway, and I turned to look, too.

Barry was there. He stood at the entrance to the room looking out of place in his jeans and work shirt and sneakers—and his youth.

There was a time I would have flinched from shame at his inappropriate clothing, but not now. Steve was right. As long as he came—that's what mattered.

He walked self-consciously to my mother. As he put his cheek against her lips, she cried against him, wetting his face with her tears. I moved past Cy and his wife to where Barry was standing. "Barry."

I put my face up to kiss him, but he didn't respond. Still angry. He stood stiffly.

Steve came into the room. He shook Barry's hand.

"I'm glad you made it. How did you get

here?" Steve asked him.

"Richie—" he glanced away from us as he said the name "—dropped me off."

"Will you be going back with us?" Steve asked him, and my heart began racing. But before Barry could answer, the somber little man was in the room announcing, "Will the immediate family please follow me into the chapel for services? And then the rest of the family and friends."

I was surrounded by some of my cousins' friends who had just come in. Barry and Steve waited for me beyond them.

"How's your family?" I was asked.

"Fine. There they are. Barry," I introduced my son. "And my boyfriend, Steve."

They greeted them and we went into the chapel shaking our heads and clucking in sympathy, yet more lighthearted for having seen one another after all those years.

Steve went into the row of benches first, deliberately putting Barry and me together. The rabbi waited for everyone to get silent, and then he started with some Hebrew prayers, and then the speech.

He called her a good woman. She was, but I wondered if he would say it if he'd known her. She was outspoken and raucous and flirtatious. She loved action and movement and fun. I don't think she had been in a synagogue once since her sons' Bar Mitzvahs.

I could picture her as she was then in a wide hat and a loose-fitting, wide-shouldered dress. "Aren't I lucky?" she had said. "I only have to go through this once."

A devoted wife. It was the standard speech. But, I suddenly thought, what could they say about me? A devoted wife? Never to Nat. I wanted nothing less than to be perfect. It was easier wanting than doing, and I soon gave up both. Even on our honeymoon, even at that impossible hotel in the Bahamas where the other guests regarded Nat as though he were a mouse scurrying around their feet, even then I remember a good-looking blond Gentile boy around my age who kept watching me and smiling at me. I never spoke to him, but those meaningful glances of his stirred up more electricity than all the contact in my marriage bed. I turned my back on the boy, but I cherished the secret of my feelings. I knew that someday . . .

Steve cleared his throat. Our eyes met. His mother had been in an institution all the years of his adolescence and youth. (Maybe that was why he found it so difficult to make friends, why he seemed to need me, as he got older, even more than I needed him.)

I had never known his mother, nor his father, for that matter. But I knew him when his father was still alive and ailing. The old man had had a girl friend. Girlfriend! What an odd name for that poor-looking woman who stood apart from the family weeping to herself at his funeral.

Steve's sister had murmured through tight lips, "Why did *she* have to come?" and she pointedly ignored her even though it was the girl friend who made their father's last years bearable.

Would that be me at Steve's funeral (God forbid) or him at mine? The idea was morbid. I tried to concentrate on what the rabbi was saying.

Adoring mother. He was talking about my Aunt Shirley, but again, I thought of myself. Devoted? Perhaps on the surface, but I knew better. (I could hear Suzanne's laugh mocking me.) At least, I should be honest with myself.

It wasn't so much that I left Barry to meet

Steve. Or that maids and baby-sitters raised him. (Once Nat came home early and found Barry standing in a clothes closet being punished for eating a cookie in his room. Still, Nat waited for me to get home and fire the maid.) That wasn't the worst, either.

It was my using him all the time—to show off with, to justify myself, to use as an excuse not to give up the comforts I enjoyed. And yet, being honest, I wasn't a terrible mother. I loved my son. I tried to understand him.

How could I hit him for being queer? No, not queer. It had a name—homosexual. How could I be so unfeeling? Maybe it was Suzanne acting as though it were a joke. It wasn't. Not for me, not for him.

In the front row of the chapel my mother was crying little wounded cries, counterpoint to the rabbi's overly cultured voice.

Everyone stood. Out of habit, I glanced at Barry to make sure he was doing the right thing. Of course, he was.

Poor Barry. To have had the burden of his secret at such an early age.

"Shirley Glick Marks." The name was startling in the midst of the Hebrew prayer. Moe was weeping in the front row. Jack put his arm around his stepfather's shoulder.

My aunt was sixty when she died. In twenty-four years, I'd be sixty. It didn't seem like such a hell of a lot. Twenty-four years ago I was twelve. I went out on my first date at twelve. I came home from the skating rink and when I looked down, the boy's hand was on my breast. I hadn't felt a thing. The boy's name was Marvin Ritter.

The pallbearers stepped up to the coffin. The mourners in the first row followed them out.

"Barry, are you planning to go to the cemetery?"

"No. My friend's picking me up here later."

"I wanted to speak to you."

"Phyllis, honey, how are you?" Some neighbors of Aunt Shirley's were standing in the aisle. They made room for Barry and Steve and me to go immediately ahead of them. And while we walked, they filled the air with their chatter.

"So sudden."

"Unexpected."

"So much fun in her."

" . . . biggest specialists . . ."

" . . . considered young today. . . ."

We were out of the chapel.

"Is that your son?"

"Oh, yes. Barry, these are some of Aunt Shirley's neighbors. You were much smaller when they last saw you."

"What a looker," one of the women gushed.

Barry's face reddened and he shifted his feet. We were back out in the bright sunlight and the oppressive heat. Traffic flowed next to us, and at the park across the street, people were walking dogs, and kids were riding bicycles. We stood clustered on our side of the street, thoughts of Shirley still binding us together.

"What did you want to ask me?" Barry asked when there was a break in the talk.

"What?"

"You said you wanted to talk to me."

I excused us and led Barry to the edge of the crowd. Steve was standing near the door to the funeral home lighting a cigarette.

"I'm sorry, Barry, for having lost my temper on Friday." I faltered. Too much emotion the whole morning. I wished Steve were right with us. Well, say it, I told myself. Let him know before he stops caring. "I love you. No matter what. Please come home."

He looked as though he had something he wanted to say, too, but I continued.

"I need you," I said.

"OK." He looked away, over my head, reminding me of the way kids answer if you ask them if they want a soda or a snack. *OK*. As if it didn't matter to them. But it mattered to Barry.

Now it was his turn to falter. He still couldn't look me in the face. "I wish you could be proud of me."

He said it so low, it was almost as though he were speaking to himself. Steve was by my side. From him, I got the strength and the will to say it. "I am, Barry. I am."

I threw an arm around my son's neck and drew his head closer so I could kiss him. He barely let me. It won't be easy, I thought. We had far to go together, my son and I.

"Is there room in your car to take two people to the cemetery?" one of the men from the funeral home asked Steve.

Please, no, I thought. I wanted to talk to Steve alone.

"We're going to be staying on the Island," Steve explained.

"That's all right," the man replied. "I can get them a ride back."

"We'll see you later?" I asked Barry.

He nodded.

An ancient couple I recognized as Moe's brother and his wife were led to us.

"The car's around the corner," Steve told them. He turned to Barry. "I'll take you out for driving practice when you come home later. OK?"

For the first time that day, my son smiled. "OK."

I took Steve's arm gratefully. He knew how to uncomplicate things.

"You're Shirley's niece, the one from Long Island. Right? That's your husband?" the old woman we were going to drive asked me about Steve. I had the feeling she knew he wasn't, but she wanted to hear my explanation.

"No. He's my boyfriend," I told her.

"You have the one boy or more?"

The questions went on as we got into the car and then as we drove through the streets of Brooklyn to the highways leading out to Long Island. Once she stopped asking questions, she went on in a monologue about her own family and then Moe. It seemed her husband had worked for Moe in the office.

"He did some managing for Moe, too. He checked on the supers."

Did she know my father had been a super? I glanced in the back to read her expression, but she kept on talking. Maybe it would occur to her or her husband later on, and then she would be embarrassed that she'd mentioned it.

What did it matter? All that vanity on my mother's part. "If anyone asks you," she used to say, "tell them your father's in real estate."

So he left his super's job and was shot in the head for his trouble. What a hard life he had, a hard thirty-four years.

On we drove, as her voice droned on about Moe and his success and her own husband's importance. Every once in a while she would turn to her husband for him to corroborate some point.

"Yeah," he'd say, and I think he dozed off until the next pause.

We were driving out on the highway that cut through the suburbs. Two gasoline stations, a motel, a supermarket, some stores devoted to cars, a diner, and we were in the next town. Finally, we turned off the main road into a less developed area. We passed some old frame houses between undeveloped lots, and a group of black kids standing around a bicycle.

Are they glad? I wondered. Another white person's funeral? They didn't look our way.

A snakelike formation of cars was lined up at the gate of the cemetery. We inched our way into the parking lot. When I opened the door, a rush of hot air hit me for a moment and settled in my stomach as nausea.

"What's the matter?" Steve asked.

"Nothing." But I held on to him as we walked. (I could be rid of this feeling so easily, I thought. A scraping, a day in bed, and I'd be my old self again.)

My mother was standing with Cy and his wife waiting for us at the end of the lot. They were talking about the family, their kids, as Shirley would have liked us to speak, as she would have spoken herself. They asked me about mine.

"Fine . . . summer school . . . learning to

drive." I asked them about theirs.

"Traveling . . . youth   group . . . dean's list . . . popular. And the other . . . summer camp . . . sports . . . good in science."

For a second, Cy's wife's eyes met mine. What secret about them was *she* keeping from *me*? It wasn't easy to be a parent. No matter how glibly we spoke for the grand-parents.

We went on the narrow path between the gravestones to the site where the mourners were gathered. My mother was told to come up front near the mound of dirt dug from her sister's grave. The rabbi began his prayers.

My mother was crying aloud now. Tears filled my eyes. What was she thinking about? Of horse-drawn wagons and the farms of Brooklyn? Of the dances they used to go to on Saturday nights where they did the Charleston and the Peabody? Of the girl she confided to after dates and scolded for borrowing her best camisole without ask-ing? The girl became a woman, an impor-tant person in my mother's life, someone to measure herself by, to measure me, too, for that matter. How much of what she told me was for Shirley's sake, to please her or impress her?

One time she didn't listen to Shirley. It was during the Depression. My father's leg had been broken in an accident and my mother had become pregnant accidentally.

Shirley, up to her elbows in diapers for the twins that had just been born, urged my mother to have the baby. "You'll manage somehow. God provides."

My mother, the sole support of the family at the time, wouldn't listen. "What was there for me to do? Go to my in-laws? Over my dead body," was the way she told it to me.

She had the abortion. "Your father" was the one she blamed it on, but the decision was hers and no one else's. And she always spoke of it afterward in a rush of emotion.

No. It wasn't as easy as *scrape, scrape, all over*. It was a human life, after all.

A deep sob tore through the crowd—Moe—and the services were finished. We made way for the mourners to go through.

Moe stepped between us, looking lost, adrift. And his stepsons, Cy and Jack, after him, both of them wet eyed, even Cy, I marveled, and then my mother.

I followed them and caught up to my

mother putting my arm through hers. She walked slowly, leaning on me.

Yes, lean on me. Draw what little comfort you can from the fact that in spite of all my impatience and criticism, and I think you sense *them*, you are my mother and I love you. You didn't have such an easy life. Who am I to judge you? If I thought you knew more than you did, if I listened too much to you, that was my mistake. I should have known better. But you never wanted anything less than what you thought was the best for me.

Jack was waiting outside the funeral car for my mother. I kissed her good-bye and Jack put out his hand to me. There was something in it.

"My mother wanted you to have it."

It was a cameo. The background was brown, the model yellowish. Three diamond chips were imbedded around her neck.

"I know this isn't the place," Jack was saying, "but I didn't want to forget it. My mother gave it to me to give to you weeks ago."

"Thank you. She was so thoughtful to remember me." I said good-bye to him choked with feeling.

I held it in my lap in the car. It was garish. At one time I thought Aunt Shirley knew all there was to know about fine things. She didn't, of course. Everything she owned was in her taste—oversized, expensive, gaudy.

I pinned the cameo to my dress. In spite of how it looked, I'd always treasure it because it was hers and she wanted me to have it.

I put my head back on the seat. We were back on the highway, the seat rocking gently, the sound of tires and wind whirring together.

"I think Barry wanted to come home all along," Steve remarked. "He wanted to be asked. And he wanted to know that you still love him."

"I'll never accept it fully, Steve. There are going to be problems."

We were sitting apart as we always did, like a married couple. I moved closer to him.

"Life is full of problems," he said.

It was true. He knew the bad ones, too. But, more rational, he looked for less in life, was satisfied with less, was more willing to wait than I. How long would he wait? It wasn't fair for me to make him wait, to deceive him, to pretend I wasn't pregnant.

Not everything can be planned out, I told myself. That was life: problems and embarrassments and unexpected joys. It might be good to have a baby—Steve's baby. He would make a wonderful father.

Why was I afraid? Was it the knowledge that all I had to do was to say it once and all my silences, all denials would be negated? Yes it was. And also the fear of being talked about, of having to change a routine, of being the oldest in the maternity ward. All that and a few sensible reasons, too. But take the chance, I thought.

And think of Steve. All the years he wanted children, he never pressed me or left me (except that once).

"What are you thinking?" he asked me as we pulled up to the house.

Take the chance. "I'll tell you inside."

I ran to open the door and throw away the note to Barry and flick the air conditioner on. We both washed our hands. ("Always wash up after you come home from the cemetery." One of the few religious injunctions we heeded.) And I threw the

199

towel we wiped them on into the hamper.

"Want coffee? Lunch?"

"OK."

It seemed right that he would remember to ask me again while he was eating a sandwich and drinking coffee. I hadn't mentioned it because the catch was still there in my throat, my heart still slowed every time I thought of it. I had been frightened for so long, I couldn't change in an instant.

No. I was afraid of marriage, but sitting at the kitchen table with him and waiting for him to ask, I felt calmer than I had since I first became overdue. Ask me, I thought. I'll tell you that I'll have your baby—our baby. You should have made me pregnant years ago when Nat died. Why did you ever put up with my neurosis? (You needed me, the truth-seeking part of my brain answered, and that was *your* neurosis.) Hell, it was easier when everything was called *love* and we let it go at that.

"What are you smiling about?" he asked. "What are you thinking?"

"Some more coffee?"

"No."

I got another cup for myself and sat next

to him taking his long bony fingers in my hand. Age spots. Some daddy.

"You know I'm impetuous," I began. "Even though we've only known each other for nineteen years . . ." I stopped. "Oh, the hell with joking around, Steve. I want to marry you."

He leaned over and kissed me gently on the lips. Nice. Not thrilling, but then I would be perfectly contented with *nice*.

"It's about time. When do you want to go for our blood tests?"

"This week. Tomorrow."

He raised an eyebrow and smiled at me quizzically. "Why the rush?"

"Don't you know?"

He shook his head.

"You must have slipped it past me. I'm a week overdue."

Now he leaned forward in his chair, showing some excitement. "Pregnant! That's great."

I got up from my seat and sat in his lap. "I want to have your baby, Steve. Maybe another after this one. Just help me. You know me—I'm scared."

"Don't be. You never really had to be."

He held me until I was completely

surrounded by his warmth—a baby myself. I closed my eyes.

There was a whole big complicated world waiting for me when I got up. No, I wasn't going to think of it. And I wasn't going to think of the past, either. It was the past that made me fearful of the future. No. I was just going to think of this moment, this second—alone and separate from past and future.